A

Starry

Eyed

A Starry Eyed

Komal Choubisa

PAPER TOWNS
PUBLISHERS

PAPER TOWNS
P U B L I S H E R S

First published by
Papertowns Publishers
72, Vishwanath Dham Colony,
Niwaru Road, Jhotwara,
Jaipur, 302012

A Starry-Eyed
Copyright © Komal Choubisa, 2021

ISBN Print Book - 978-93-91228-82-8

Cover Design by Aditi Shah
Instagram Id: @the.book.story
aditicshah01@gmail.com

Printed in India

To those who love their parents
&
To those who dare to dream

Dedication:

To, My Parents (The world's best people).
This book is for you.

Author's Note

First of all, I would like to say thanks to all my readers.

I was somewhere between a naïve girl and a dreamer. I live on my own terms and always try to catch flights and not emotions *(trying my best)*. Exploring the world is my passion. I feel I am on cloud 9 when I read books during my long-haul flights. Professionally, I worked with an Airline consolidator (IATA accredited firm). I encourage women empowerment.

An ambitious, talented girl, I was brought up listening to fairy tales and was always one who curiously believed in them. I am not the sort of girl who gives up on anything so quickly. I want everything from my life. Despite facing several obstacles, I have been working hard to achieve my goals. I live in dreams, and they are everything for me. My biggest mantra to life is 'Nothing Is Impossible'.

Dream big and never regret doing things you always wished to as long as you are not harming anyone. Follow your passion & live the life that you have always wanted to, even if others don't understand it. It is hard to please everyone. They will always judge you no matter what.

Each coin has two sides. One side made me feel on cloud nine & the other side of the coin showed me its unpredictable phase & shit happened. My life was somehow becoming a roller coaster ride. At one time, I was a bundle of mischief, unknowingly stuck within the catastrophe. And somewhere, I almost lost my working path. I learned a lot in the time of my setback. An idle mind is the devil's playground, and I dealt with that shit.

I believe in the value of family, self-love, working lifestyle, integrity, health, simplicity, self-discipline, positive vibes, cerebral work and stick-to-it-iveness.

It's no exaggeration that life gave me a second chance to live. Once again, I found life calling, and it made me an author. I wrote this book not because I have attained some great intelligence and feel qualified to edify but because I want to write stories through my life experiences. If my existence no longer remains on the earth, then I want to leave my words behind for the world. Maybe for some good change. I have been exploring the world & simultaneously learning life on my own. Hence I would love to call myself a student of life.

Love' n Luck
KC

A personal message for all the women out there:

Being feminine is a precious gift. Never let equality fool you to lose your femininity. Be well-educated & enjoy womanhood while chasing your rights, responsibilities and dreams.

Words of wisdom

- Don't be upset about your failure. You are still a step ahead of those who don't even try.
- Never cry in front of anyone except your parents. They are the only ones who know the worth of your tears.
- Never lie to your parents (it will cost you a lot, much later).
- Toxic People always judge, no matter what you do. It's part of their job. Learn how to prepare your mind to ignore their bullshit.
- First, achieve your goals, work for your dreams, make your parents proud. Then fall in love for the rest of your life. Be Committed to your Dreams and Goals.
- No one can stand up to fight for you and change your life except yourself.
- There should be no blame game. You are the only one responsible for your success and failure.
- Yes, we all make mistakes, no one is perfect as we are human, and one day we all will die, so our mistakes vanish with us as well. So, make mistakes, forgive yourself, learn from them, and move on gently. The point is to scrutinize mistakes and be the best version of yourself.

- People who bully and pass negative comments are just distractions. Giving a damn will ultimately be leading you to failure.
- Never think by Heart (emotions) but by Brain (intelligence).
- Do what you love to do. Otherwise, you will be betraying none other than yourself.
- Never ask anything from anyone, except your parents. Free is too expensive.
- Big No-No, to trust anyone, except your parents and instinct.
- The problem is not that big as we create it in our minds. Throughout every trouble, communication with the right person is the key.
- Real Success is what includes Health + Happiness.
- A Life itself is a success. One should celebrate it.
- Life is a precious gift from God. Learn to live every second of it without holding any grudges. Why waste the priceless moments of your life judging, bullying and spreading hate and negativity. We are all born with unique qualities & live once, so make it worth living. We live every day and die once. Make every day count.

Chapter 1

A Fantasy

17th July 2007. She was sitting on an organic cotton abstract newspaper printed Sacco chair bought from Italy, oft looking at the wall clock as if she was waiting for something vital. It was around 2:00 am as per Kuala-Lumpur (Malaysia) time zone. Silence reached its peak.

A teenager with messy long curly blonde hair and hazel eyes seemed to be stuck in the middle of the road. She was wearing a red beret with the word "Bonjour" written on it. Lilac grey sweatshirt with a jet black knee-length expensive overcoat having ancient golden buttons. Black skinny jeans and face half-covered with a chunky white knit scarf wrapped around her neck & shoulder. Walking with bleeding bare feet on white snow in -2 degree temperature, trying to flag down a cab, but they were all full. She kept walking straight towards the thoroughfare for almost an hour till she reached the riverbank.

'How tranquil this place is!' She whispered.

She got exhausted and sat down in a corner. Wanting to light a cigarette, she dug into her pockets to pull out a matchbox or lighter if there were any. Suddenly, a male voice came from behind her, "Smoking cigarettes is injurious to health". She shrugged & turned around.

A 6'1" tall, dark man was standing behind her. His red eyes were only visible in the darkness. He kept staring intensely into her eyes as if he was familiar with or had known her for donkey's years. He was in an extraordinary rig-out. She curiously asked.

"Who are you?"

"Truth or Lie?"

"Obvio, Truth."

"A 17 yrs. ago dead man."

"Lol, don't you think you sound unreal? I told you to tell me the truth. Who are you?"

"I revealed the truth only."

"Unbelievable!"

"However, I can tell you that you are a true human being because you don't believe in my honesty. I know 99% of humans believe in fake."

"I don't think so. Well, what brings you here?"

"First, tell me, why aren't you horror-struck from me? That's quite peculiar to me."

"If you are not lying, you are less noxious than a human being. I, too, want to be dead soon."

"Want to die! Beauty like an English Rose just alive to die. Strange, isn't it?"

"Well, this rose has several thorns. I want to ignite this beauty. It is a curse or grace, and I have no clue about it."

"Oh, stop saying anything infelicitous about yourself. Your beauty is an honour. Ask those who are physically challenged and living happily like no one else. You should be grateful for your life, moron."

Tears rolled down her cheeks.

"Stop Boohooing. I didn't mean to hurt you. I apologise if I behaved rudely. I know every girl on the planet deserves to be treated like a queen. I should have learnt it."

"Life isn't trouble-free among the bloodthirsty, especially to a girl like me. Might be I am not a blessed child."

"Aren't you overthinking?"

"No, of course not. My stepmother never accepted me as her daughter. I was living as a tenant in my own house. My alcoholic Dad lost his life due to an alcohol overdose, and I was the reason. I don't even know why people consume alcohol! What's wrong with healthy fruit juices! Coconut water & natural water per day! What do you say?"

"You never tried alcohol?"

"Did I say that? Yes, I drank on the day when I completed my higher education. I got bad grades, so my haters bullied me. To get over all these, my dad took us on holiday. I took my first sip of alcohol while sitting at the beach with my Dad. He got overdrunk, as usual. His lungs were already half damaged, and he lost his life when we were on vacation. I hardly get joyful moments, and if anyone tries to give me a ray of joy, it turns into a tragic day by itself. I could not accept that we went on vacation to collect good memories, and they turned into bad memories. How can I say that I am not cursed."

"I still can say that you are not."

"My stepmother knew I had aquaphobia and didn't know how to swim. It was a perfect day to make hay while the sun shines for my stepmother. She threw me in the middle of the ocean when I lost my father. A lady with a red mark on her face saved my life. I disliked her at first glance because of the ugly red mark on her forehead. But later, she saved my life. I was indebted to her. I got to know the meaning of humanity and inner beauty. I drank the second time when my Dad left nothing for me in his will. 3rd time was when I was missing my biological mother. If I get caught drinking, it can be reckoned that I am in great misery. The 4th is never going to have happened because I left it forever. Whenever I drink, I feel brain dead. I pray every day to God to forgive my sin. Honestly, it was all not planned. I didn't want to as it happened inflow. Moreover, I hate those who consume alcohol, no offence, but it's worst for the human being and health."

"What about your stepmother? Why doesn't she love you?"

"I don't know, but my stepmother never allowed me to buy new clothes or to go outside with friends and colleagues. No perfume and makeup for me. I love fashion. I was treated like a maid in my own house. I worked in a coffee shop adjoined by my home building. On x-mas I tried to spoil myself with expensive clothes and went to a movie with my one male colleague because he asked me to do so. I couldn't say no."

"Because you needed someone in your life."

"I couldn't comment on it because he told me he was a gay. I respect that he had enough courage to confront it. He was good looking and brilliant and belonged to Manhattan, New York City. He came here just to explore a new culture. I respect him as I believe in humanity. I support the LGBT community. I wonder why people can't treat each other equally. Live and Let Live. Life is beautiful."

"Even I respect, but I want to know, am I interacting with a lesbian for so long?"

"Well, I support the LGBT community, but unfortunately, I am straight without having any boyfriend."

"Thank God, you are single."

"Don't forget you are dead. Stop acting like a 'Don Juan'.
"Men will be Men."

"Lol, when I returned home after celebrating x-mas, my mother vacated my room. I was asked to go anywhere, but I wasn't allowed to live with them. I was bowing & scraping to be at home where I belong to, I apologised, but I couldn't make up her mind. I lost my job as well. My senior replaced me with a Russian Boy without letting me know. I didn't even know the reason why they fired me."

"Your nominal mother played her best role."

"Maybe, your prediction is on the mark, but I don't want to blame anyone. Even I believe in giving blessings to my haters. I left home, and I dossed down on the pavement hiding my cursed face."

"Wai…..wait a sec. What did I again hear? Cursed face! Why do you consider yourself jinxed? You aren't."

"I don't know, I couldn't sleep because of starvation. I dug into my pocket to pull out coins, but I had no single penny. A homeless person was playing the guitar on the same street & looking at me mercifully. He gave me a packet of cigarettes to lessen my starvation. I refused to receive it as it wasn't appropriate for me to take anything from a stranger. He forcefully kept it in my pocket."

"You are like my best friend. You can take anything from me. I spent my entire money, even I lost my shoes, so I can't help. I can't even sell my guitar, as it does not belong to me. You can use one cigarette whenever you feel hungry, but promise me you won't buy another packet. I am afraid you would get addicted like me. I smoke it every day because I am addicted." Homeless said.

"I put him on one condition that I would only accept one packet of the cigarettes if he takes my shoes, and he locked the deal. I gave him my favourite unisex boots to reciprocate his affection. He broke down while wearing it, 'What a perfect pair!' saying it, he smiled at me." She continued,

"The apex thing about this guy was, he wasn't wealthy, just a homeless. However, he respected and addressed me as his best friend. He wasn't craving for my curves and white body. He helped me selflessly. He touched my heart because I have met only rapacious people to date. I felt myself in 7th heaven when he said: I was like his best friend. He gave me a packet of cigarettes *(I am not recommending anyone to smoke. Smoking cigarettes causes cancer)*. Because it was the only thing he had left, to give and to show his kindness. Isn't it heart wrenching? That was when I got to know the value of food, the actual meaning of poverty, and how it feels to be starved! I promised myself that I would never disrespect food by disliking its taste."

"How did you get wounded? Why bleeding feet?"

"Again, a long story would explain in terse. Few street goons threw glass bottles because I bruised their ego. I donated my boots to a tramp who was in need. Maybe those nincompoops wanted my boots, or they didn't like my compassionate attitude. They came along chasing me halfway and made me frightened.

"You just made up a story."

"It's not my strawberry week," She retorted, rolling her eyes.

"They were just misogynists."

"Maybe, however, I eschew being in a crowd."

"I just created a thought in my mind after seeing you, if I were not dead, I would have married you to keep you protected for a lifetime, but I am sure you would have rejected me."

"Lol, What was your dream at that time, when you were alive & kicking?"

"I had many, but I always wanted gender equality, world peace & to stop racism."

"I appreciate it, but I am not a racist. Would you mind if I ask how you got killed?"

"Life is always at stake in the military."

"You are a black man with a golden heart."

"How did you get to know my surname was Blackman?"

"I mean, your skin colour is dark, and you are kind-hearted."

"I can reveal your thoughts as I can sniff your mind."

"What?"

"The thought running in your mind as of now is, 'why can't people keep minding their own business?' Am I right? Am I right?"

"Damn, right."

"Destiny would protect you from death once in your life."

"How sure are you?" She blurted

"You unknowingly sat on my grave."

"Oh! Dammit!"

"That's fine, "I've got a gift for you," He disappeared.

It's a leaf, an oakleaf with something written on it, "La Vie Est Belle, but why did he give me this?" She stalled.

It was something that touched her feet. It was a mongoose. She got horrified & scared. Meanwhile, she gazed at the multitudinous broken bones, a skeleton lying on the muddy ground, weird, squeaky voices coming from behind her back as if someone was calling her name. Someone pulled her hair badly. She screamed and ran away.

Chapter 2

Roused

17th July 2007. Abruptly the landline phone rang. She got up hurriedly, looking at her surroundings. She was slightly scared, and her palm was trembling. She looked at the wall clock. It was 4 o'clock as per Kuala-Lumpur (Malaysia) time zone. She touched her forehead with her trembling palm and breathed a sigh of relief, "Oh lord! I was dog-tired while waiting for their text message, and I drifted off on Sacco chair. What a nightmare it was! Who was that mysterious girl in my dream? And that Ghost, a 17yrs ago dead, fear and spookiness, isn't it? Thank god it was just a nightmare as I didn't interact with any ghost. Let me pinch myself that I am alive."

The telephone was ringing continuously.

"Who would be ringing the telephone at this time? It might be something on high priority," She muttered.

She got up and picked up the telephone.

"Hello, Speak up; your voice is not audible. May I know who is calling me? H..hello?" Since no one was answering the call, she put down the receiver.

Her doorbell rang. "Who could it be at this time! What's happening here!" She whispered.

She walked towards the door and tried to see outside through an eye hole. Nobody was standing there.

The doorbell was ringing endlessly. She wanted to go to open the door, but she thought, 'What if someone came to kill me or to steal something from the house?' It was possible as Khwahish was an independent girl, she was living solely alone. She moved to her kitchen, dug into a drawer to pull out a knife. However, she didn't want to be too violent, so she decided to carry a butter knife along with her while opening the door. She went towards the main gate and opened it ferociously.

She looked in all directions, but no one was there. As she came inside, the doorbell rang again, "Who is doing all this! What do they want! Who is this flapdoodle! Playing a threatening game with a girl like a Lily Livered!" She was frightened.

Minutes later, she yelled from inside, "Whoever you are, come outside, or I would call the cops. (paused) Should I call the cops now?"

Meantime, the telephone rang. Standing in the middle of the hallway, she thinks, 'where should I go? To open the door, pick up the telephone, or check the closet for some extremely important work. Obvio! Work is important." She had no courage to face the situation. She neglected the whole scary scenario and was about to move to her room to find something in the wardrobe. By the skin of her teeth, she half proceeded towards her room, but the repeated ringing of the telephone was disturbing her.

She picked up the call: "Hello, Hello"…..

Since it was nobody, she lost her temper and yelled over the blank dialer, "Who is this? What do you want? Why can't you speak up? You must have a lot of time for all this nonsense, but I don't." She hung up the phone in aggression.

As she headed towards her room where her closet was lying, the telephone rang again, and she quickly received it.

"Who is this?!"

"Hey! This is your Granny, all the way from the USA."

"Granny! Who?"

"Your Mother's Mother."

"Oh, thanks for an explanation, but did you give me several blank calls? You did all that crap to make me scared? Seriously!........Well, nothing more to be expected from a mean-spirited person. Anyway, could I ask something, 'Your Highness'?

"Yes, Of course! You can ask me anything, I am all ears, but I have one condition."

"Condition! What Condition?"

"That you will stop behaving formally to me. I am your Granny. I am expecting you to address me by this name."

"Doesn't matter, why blank calls at this time? Do you know what time it is here? It's 04:30 here. I grievously got scared."

"Why are you getting pissed off?"

"Because you deserve it, simple."

She pretended as though she had no idea what had happened, "My innocent grandchild, I don't even know what you are talking about & why are you behaving like this? It wasn't to make you scared. I had a word with your mamma the last evening, and your Mamma gave me this number. May I know where you live in Kuala-Lumpur?"

"Gosh! Too innocent, Momsy." *Whispered*

"Yes, despite knowing the fact you don't want to talk to me, I tried my fate. I yearned for you; therefore, I couldn't restrict myself for so long, I didn't even see the time, and dialled your number without fail. Moreover, it wasn't a blank call, sweetie. I lost my mobile phone while grocery shopping. My telephone has not been operating well for the last week; hence it might be possible I wasn't audible at that time. A genuine guy found my phone & returned it a few minutes back."

"Just Grow up! I am least interested in what had happened in the grocery store last night! Why did you call me on this landline if you already have my mobile number?"

"I do have, and I saved both your numbers with the same name on my mobile phone. So, I didn't check what number I was dialling on."

"Just an excuse."

"First, I thought seeing my number on your phone screen, you won't bother to answer."

"Don't be worried about it. I had no number belonging to you saved in my phone & I do answer random strangers' calls as well, maybe someone in need."

"Would you please stop retorting & shut your mouth for a second? Would you stop behaving like an angry bird? Let's postpone this fight sequence for another day. Could I ask you to give me seven kisses like you used to do when you were a toddler? I have been craving for your love for ages."

"Big NO! When I was a toddler, I didn't know what you did to my Momsy, Your Highness. If I were aware of what you did, I would have never let anyone talk to you."

"I am not a witch."

"Not even less than, … I beg your pardon! Your Highness! might hurt your ego!"

"I hardly believe in being egotist, and why have you been addressing me, 'Your Highness'? Why are you getting mad at me? What's the matter? Why can't you address me, 'Granny'?"

"You belong to a wealthy King family. I saw a dream in my childhood that I earwigged talking to someone over the phone. It was your relative. It might be your brother. And no one bothered to let me know about its veracity. Despite asking several times, none tells me anything about our Family. I only got to know that when my Momsy needed you, you left her alone to struggle financially and emotionally. Why couldn't you help her! How brutal!"

"It was nothing like that as it seems to you."

"I saw my mother struggling alone forever and a day! Did you hate her so much that you couldn't be there in her tough times! She was alone, moreover, you left her when she needed you the most."

"I feel proud and blessed that I gave birth to a pure, innocent soul on this planet. How would I hate her?"

"Are you joking with me, or do you mean it?"

"I mean it. Your mother is my Gold."

"Then why did you leave her? I want to know everything about us."

"Surely I will tell you everything, but I need one promise."

"Promise! What promise?"

"That, you would call me 'Granny', not 'Your Highness', and gimme the seven kisses."

"I would love to call you Granny if you agreed to pour your heart out to let me know everything about our family. And don't ask me to give you the seven kisses, for heaven's sake. I will never do it for you at any cost. I am sorry, but you lost that respect. A moment ago, you scared me, and in the next moment, you are asking me for the precious seven kisses. How diplomatic! You left my Momsy when she needed you the most. My Momsy almost could have died. Do you still think you deserve my seven kisses? C'mon, grow up. You are not my love anymore."

"Your such behaviour is killing me."

"I don't care, and for heaven's sake, promise me something that you would never make late-night calls ever again in the future, Or I am telling you right at this moment, I would surely depart the world. That time the whole situation was exceedingly life-threatening. I could have died due to shock by your blank calls, Granny."

"Yeah, I promise, but I want to know, did I solely frighten you? A heroic girl like you? If yes, then I won," Granny postulated.

"It's a safe country, but the scene you created was scary. I felt scared badly. Those 30 minutes, I thought a serial killer entered my house, and I was going to die, but it was just negative energy."

"Okay, can't you forgive me?"

"Maybe a granddaughter can, but a daughter can never forgive you."

"Please, don't...s.. ay thi…s."

"Can we change the topic, or I should address, Your Highness again?"

"No, better change the topic."

"Well, what perfect timing! I must say. I was waiting for my flight. I got a message that it has been delayed. Can you guess? What was I going to do before getting your call?"

"How would I know! Well, what were you going to do? Tell me, and I would know, then." *Nervous*

"I was about to open the closet to pull the photo album."

"Photo album! My photo album! I don't know what photo album are you talking about? Why is my photo album with you?" Granny asked surprisingly.

"I do apologize from the bottom of my heart. Let me elaborate my sentiments to you. Wrap your head around it. I stole it while leaving the house. I am sorry."

"Stole! Now you are making my blood boil," Granny said aggressively.

"It's nothing like getting your blood boiled. It's just a storm in a teacup. I had stolen from the old wooden closet that grandpa gifted you on your wedding anniversary. Momsy never allowed me to look at a single fraction of it. Neither does she tell me anything about my father and our family, nor you. Where and who is my father? No one cares about my curiosity, so I had no option left except this. I want to know about all of you, about our parted family. I am remorseful. I take the lid off what I did was felonious. It's all because of my love for my family. Everyone has a right to know about their family. So, I tried my best, therefore make me free to look at it. By the way, Granny, did you ever installed a hidden camera at our house or here to spy? How your timing is always so perfect!"

"Lol." *Granny grinned*

"Please, permit me to see all those photographs. You know exactly what they mean to me?"

"Curiosity killed the cat."

Forthwith, her phone beeped with a message tone.

"Oh, Dammit! It got cancelled. Not again, don't get it cancelled, please," *whispered*, a message made her aggravated.

"What got cancelled?"

"My flight got cancelled due to bad weather. It's rainy season here. All the flights have been delayed or cancelled these days. I have nothing to do for the whole day except being in this room and listening to you. Granny, you know what? I don't admire it. I loathe staying home throughout the day."

"Sweetie, what are you doing there in Malaysia? You are all alone. You don't need to be vexatious with your professional life. I would be unable to sleep thinking and worrying about you. Your mama and I are there to protect and help you financially. By god's grace, we have the necessary capital to live off and survive."

14

"I appreciate your emotional contribution to date. However, how long would you do this to me, Granny?" She replied sarcastically.

"Not again"

"Okay, I apologise. I like to be independent. I should contribute financially to my elders instead of still being dependent on Momsy. I felt it was wrong. It's not me. It's not your Khwahish's principle. Life itself is a precious gift from the almighty god. It is like a miracle. I should value it, so I keep my life serene, my health and happiness above all. I count my blessings every day and make progress. I try to improve myself. I just don't want to breathe. I want to live and be financially independent to get my freedom to live the way I want to. In this era, to understand this is as simple as knowing how to cut the cake. Now onwards, don't interfere in my professional life. It's a humble request."

"What a mature woman you have become! You already make me feel so proud. I already appreciate it, but what about your marriage?"

"I know you are concerned about my safety, my well-being, and to see me standing near a fancy, decorative car bonnet tagged, 'Just Married', outside of a 5-star banquet hall. The number of guests, who would seem least interested in Bidai, but what ingredients were missing in continental dishes, could write an essay on it, I mean seriously! Who doesn't want to be a stunning bride? Everyone feels 7th heaven on their wedding day but what after that? What if I am accidentally stuck in a toxic relationship for a lifetime? After a few years of marriage, we both would earn a higher amount of our salary just to pay a psychiatrist for therapy or afford an expensive lawyer's fees. What an expensive misery, what a concept of ruining the time and wealth, isn't it?"

"So, you're never going to give us a chance to "au revoir" like that!"

"Ooh la la, French! I love it. Granny, you aged but still didn't stop learning. Well, Who doesn't want to get married? I am keen to get married. I am not against 'the blessed knot' a divine, pure ritual, but who thinks like that? Despite knowing there is no perfect match in the world, I need one for me who behaves like a gentleman. I need a perfect match for me, with whom I can feel comfortable at home, no tricky, sugar-coated, manipulative words, no love-bombings, which is so dangerous than death—someone who allows me to be independent and appreciates my ambitions. Forsooth, I want a guy who takes my dignity as his pride, who keeps his ego aside and celebrates my success rather than envy it. A guy who loves my dreams from the bottom of his heart, who never use abusive language, not even a single word. I know many guys use foul language to look cool or to feel superior, how a real man can abuse using words of respectable mother and sister transforming into worst words. ('Can't even imagine in my wildest dreams' *whispered*) using it in routine lives as it becomes so necessary calling it out of frustration because a man doesn't cry. What an excuse, bullshit, isn't it? Granny, you know what? Those who use abusive words are indirectly insulting their upbringing. A real man doesn't commit violence to a GIRL, an innocent girl. I don't want a cool guy with an ego who is keen to make a relationship with a girl who ignores him the most. I know, they take it as a challenge like it's mandatory to win a trophy, how relationships become like a game. Maybe she has been ignoring them because she doesn't want a relationship or isn't ready for it. She, too, has her own life, the same as they have. She too wants to make her parents proud, same as they want to, she too wants to achieve her dreams and goals, that's why she has been rejecting them, Oh! I am sorry I shouldn't have said it. (I bruised their ego). She has been ignoring you because she has no interest in being in a relationship as of now."

Continued…. "She is smart, therefore doesn't want to make things deliberately ugly, so she can't go against her feelings and fake them just to satisfy their ego. She respects their feelings and manhood; whether they are a powerful guy, a son of a top gun in the town or belong to a privileged background, it doesn't matter to her at all. She only gives a damn to her independence. A real guy who has enough sense would selflessly mentor her to make her parents proud. A guy who has enough courage to accept my "NO" as a compliment, unlike someone who started using foul words on being ignorant. Like an act of revenge. How can a mature mindset believe in revenge? Even more than that, acid attack & whatnot. I heard many stories like that. How would I tie a knot with an emotionally unavailable guy when I need him the most. How cruel. Granny, I won't marry anyone until I become a successful independent woman and get an honourable position in society. I want a guy who respects my independence rather than feeling inferior in front of me. I want equality in my relationship, or better, I would live single. At least I'd be happy."

"Oh my gosh! You wear your heart on your sleeve. What a lengthy lecture! Don't get yourself hot under the collar."

"If she wants to fly, give her wings, not a cage."

"Okay, sweetie, who am I to cut your wings if you have already decided to fly high."

"Better"

"Where do you live in Kuala-Lumpur, can I ask?"

"Granny, it's an apartment."

"All I want is you to take care of yourself, have all your meals on time. Don't go on a crash diet; in your case, you are already so slim and fit like a fashion model."

"Okay! Granny, Thank You."

Chapter 3

An Inquisitive

*H*er doorbell rang. Repeatedly…

"That's the last straw. Granny, hold a minute; someone is there at the door. Somebody's ringing the doorbell, hold on, give me two minutes, I will be right back," Khwahish's voice was quivering, she opened the door. One girl, dark-skinned, curly hair, 5'1", stood in front of the main gate and wiped her tears with a floral handkerchief.

It was her maid, standing right in front of her.

"Sakura! What brings you here? Look at the time!"

Sakura started sobbing.

"Sakura, what's the matter! why are you crying?"

"Ma'am, I need a day off."

"Sakura, please try to understand as we have already so much mess in the house."

"Ma'am, I know, but my son met with an accident. He is admitted to the hospital. I came here twice and rang your doorbell earlier also. I assumed that you must have been sleeping, I didn't want to ruin your sleep, so I left. I am frequently getting calls from the hospital. I have to leave now.

I need a leave, ma'am. I don't know when I will be able to come back to work."

"Oh, so it was you. You scared me out of my wits. You guys would kill me someday. Anyway, if there is an emergency, still you can't leave."

"Ma'am, you are not like that."

"Wait a minute". Khwahish moved inside her room and came outside holding an envelope, and she handed it over to Sakura, "You can't leave without taking it".

"Ma'am, this is for?"

"This is your salary, your own hard-earned money, keep it with you and consider it as an advance payment. I know you would need it."

"Thank you, Ma'am. I thought how cruel you have become! you are always an angel."

"Hey! That's fine. My feet are still on the ground. Just look after your son, alright?"

Khwahish closed the door and came inside. She picked the receiver back, "Hello? Hello? Granny...Granny, you there?" Their call got disconnected on the landline.

She went to the kitchen to make some coffee. She was fond of black coffee without sugar. Thirty minutes later, she got a call over her mobile phone. She answered the call. It was her Granny again.

"Granny, why did you disconnect the call that time!"

"I had lost myself in flashback memories. Who was it at your door!"

" It was my maid; she needed a day off, as she won't be able to come in the morning for work. She had some emergency, so she left."

"Emergency! What emergency?"

"Forget all this, none of your business. Let's get back to the point. Please allow me to see those photographs, as you

19

promised. I have been so curious to know about our family. I asked Momsy many times, but she makes excuses and gives a mysterious smile, nothing else. No one tells me the fact. I want to know."

"My grandchild, my sweetie, calm down. What do you want to know?"

"EVERYTHING, about our family, your and my Momsy's past," *curious*

"Being honest with you, your mother and my intentions were not to hide anything about all of us, as there was nothing to hide, trust me. We both just didn't want to recall the past. Your mother seems strong because she puts so much restriction on all of you. But she is vulnerable inside."

"Vulnerable? Don't use this word for women. No women on the earth are vulnerable. A woman gives birth to a life. How strong she is, isn't she? A woman can never be vulnerable. She can pretend to be weak due to her circumstances, but she can never be one of them."

"Yes, 'Fortune favours the bold', but we faced hard times, sweetie. Your mother had a heart-wrenching past. Let bygones be bygones,"

"Your Highness, not again, no more excuses. I am anxious to find out the truth."

"Okay, don't start getting mad at me again. I just didn't want to make you upset. However, you are a mature girl now. I will pour my heart out to you if you are insisting and so curious. You are a free soul like a bird. You live your life fully—a free spirit. I am sure that after knowing everything, you would surely get an emotional touchdown. If you have some patience and time to listen to the entire bygones. I would love to tell you everything."

continued…..

Chapter 4

An Ancient Era

*I*t was the time of the year 1925. There was a small village in north India with beautiful nature scenes, surrounded by sublime mountains, fresh air and quiet life. A couple were living in the village name Gopika-Nand their age around 32-35. They were wealthy farmers and had acres of land. They both were living in a riverside, at a conspicuous tree house which was a man-made treehouse, built in the year 1910 by Nand with the help of his close friend Raghuvendra. He was a best friend to Nand; they both met first in 1909 when Nand visited Kerala with Gopika as she wanted to see an Asian Elephant Calf. Raghuvendra lived in Kerala.

On 28th August 1909

They reached Kerala by railway at 7:10 pm. On arrival, they lost a receipt. On that receipt, an address was written where they were about to stay. They both were worried about where they would stay? Whom to ask for help?

They were pretending not to look worried. Their fearful emotions were clearly visible in their facial expression. They couldn't even tell anyone, as all were strangers to them. They knew no one in Kerala.

One stranger was staring at them continuously. He came closer, took their luggage, and ran away. He was running in front of their eyes, but Nand didn't do anything. Gopika shouted at Nand, "Please take some help, stop that rascal." And Nand just kept staring at him. He didn't even try to stop him. Five minutes later, they see the thief coming towards them back, but with empty hands.

"Look! he is coming towards us, but empty-handed, "Where is the luggage! Call someone to stop him right now; what are you looking at?"

When the thief came closer, she gets aggressive, "Who are you? How dare you to take our luggage without permission and run like that? Where is the luggage?"

He Looked at Nand, "Sir, I was on the same train. I came here to offer you help. Please come with me."

Gopika interrupted, "Who is this guy? We should not go with him, and we can't trust a stranger. I am scared. Please take me home back. I don't want to go further."

"Ma'am, I am not a thief, just calm down and relax. Your luggage is safely reaching my home in a Bullock cart. It was too late. I had to run because that guy couldn't wait for so long. And your luggage was so heavy, and I had to find a safe place for it. My home is just ten minutes away from here. We can go on foot. Please trust me. You can stay at my home."

"Yeah, but why are you helping us?" Nand was surprised.

"Ma'am and Sir, when you both reached here, it was so crowded, one receipt fell on the floor from your pocket. I mistakenly spilt some water while drinking it on the floor and the paper receipt. The receipt was important to you but destroyed by me. I am sorry. All I need is a chance to repent."

"I appreciate your help, but we can't stay at your home. We'll go back to our village by tomorrow. Don't insist now; you repented your mistake. We forgave you. Please get the luggage back to us."

"Sir, I am like your son. I want to tell you. It's a Sunday tomorrow."

"Yes, we know it, so?"

"I mean, we have one Festival, Thiruvonam. It will be more fun if you celebrate this auspicious occasion with us."

Nand looked at Gopika because she was too frightened.

"Ma'am, just relax. I am not a thief. I am like your son, came to help you." He was trying to comfort Gopika.

"Son! Well, we don't have any kids yet. Anyway, we can trust you now."

"Let's Go," *Finally, approved by Nand, they started moving towards his Home.*

"Sir, but why didn't you call anyone from the group of Peeler to arrest me? The way I took your luggage, it was wrong."

"You want us to call them, now?"

"No-No, Sir, I was just asking the reason."

"Peeler? I didn't even scream out loud. I was standing consciously right there when you came closer to take the luggage. I was observing your face, and you had a grin on your face that time. And the way you ran away, somewhere I got you that you were not a thief," He continued…"What a compassionate heart. You are helping strangers at an unknown place. You are a true angel for us. What's your name?"

"Sir, This is Madhavan"

"Okay, Madhavan, I think we finally reached your home as I can see a bullock cart outside your home with our luggage ."

"Yeah, that's my home. Come inside. Let me introduce you to everyone."

"That's my father. Meet my younger sister Bella and my father's cousin. You will have to share a room with him. Raghuvendra, who was born and brought up in Puducherry, relocated here to live with us and help my father in our family business. Raghuvendra is the epitome of talent. He can do whatever you ask him to do, and he would do it with perfection. He even joined French school in Puducherry and can speak French fluently."

"Quite Impressive, Raghuvendra, you will have to take us for a promenade around divine Kerala tomorrow, a heaven on earth," Nand said.

"Especially, the Elephant Calf," Gopika screamed from inside the room.

Next Day, on the occasion of Thiruvonam.

"Hey! Good Morning, Bella. What are you designing on the floor? It's amazing,"

"Good Morning, Ma'am, as it's Onam, the most important and popular National festival, especially in Kerala. This is our tradition to create a beautiful "Pookalam" on this occasion. You can wear my mum's beautiful white saree on this occasion."

"You speak so adequately, but where is your mother? Is she not helping you here?"

Bella remained silent for five minutes, as she doesn't want to let Barkha know about her sadness, but she couldn't hide her tear, that has melted in 'Pookalam.'

"Hey, what happened to you all of sudden! Did I say something wrong to you?"

Her breath caught in her throat, "My mother is no longer with us. She left us a few months back, so we are merely celebrating it, but we all are not happy. I woke up early to create a beautiful 'Pookalam', the Flower design that I created was one of my Mum's most favourite designs."

"Oh, God! I am sooo….sorry, but I am just like your mother. You can ask me for any help if you want."

"Sure, how kind you are! But I can't take your help as you are my guest. My mom taught me, 'Guests are equivalent to God'."

"I am sure she was phenomenally beautiful."

"Yes, she was. She had long black hair."

"That's amazing."

"Ma'am, I would share with you my mumma's secret of long hair."

"Okay, my Bella, so nice of you."

"Ma'am, is your name Gopika?"

"Yes!"

"I think someone is calling your name outside."

"Oh yeah, maybe for the excursion. I have to leave now. Bella, you are the most kind-hearted person I've ever met. My husband and I are so glad for the hospitality, and you have such a lovely family. We are grateful."

"Yeah, I feel so blessed sometimes, and you're most welcome, ma'am."

"Could you please raise your palm as if you are receiving a blessed food?"

"Excuse me, for what?"

She opened an ancient, beautiful gold bangle out of her one arm, gave it to Bella, and asked her to wear it.

"Ma'am, it's so expensive and beautiful. I love it. I respect your emotions, but I am so sorry, I can't receive it. We are simple people."

"Bella, you are gold-hearted, but would you deny if your mother would have given it?

You know what? We don't have any kids, so accept it. I would feel as if I am giving it to my daughter. I always want to have a baby girl, an adorable daughter like you. Please consider it as my blessings to you."

25

"Okay, Thank you Maa, I will miss you."

"Bye-Bye Bella"

Nand and Gopika returned from Kerala with beautiful memories. On Raksha Bandhan, Nand called Raghuvendra at his house to celebrate the festival altogether as Gopika went to live at her childhood friend's house for a short duration. Nand wanted to surprise his wife, so he invented an idea with the help of his friend. Nand has nothing else to do except adoring his wife to spoil her with lots of surprises and treat her like a Queen. Even though the couple had everything an average person could dream for, still they didn't have kids yet. To have one kid was their last wish remaining. Be it a girl or a boy. It was obvious for them as well to think like that. At least, they need someone to look after their wealth when they leave the world—the bitter truth of death.

Chapter 5

A Baby Cry

On 01st December 1928, early in the morning, Nand woke up and saw that Gopika was not in her room. He searched for her in the entire house, and he travelled outside to ask the neighbours if they had seen her. She was nowhere. He got tired of searching for her. At last, he sat in the corner, sitting on a stone wall gazing at the mud road. He scrutinized that mud ground had a mark of deeper barefoot prints. He got up and started following the patterns. Those prints went to the end of the mountain. After following the footprints, he reached the end. What he saw was shocking. He felt the ground slipping under his feet. He saw Gopika sitting on the precipice thoughtfully as if she was talking to kids.

"Hey!! I left no stone unturned, and you are here?"

"Just stay away, don't interrupt my children and me, let me spend time with them."

"Where are your kids? We don't have any. Let's go home?"

"You can never feel it as I do, those birds are flying in the sky, raindrops through clouds, these tiny little pebbles lying on the ground, those fishes diving deep under the oceans, all are my children, and I feel so blessed being surrounded by all of them here. I come here every day after you leave for your work. I had to hide it, as I didn't want you to know about it."

"I see eye to eye. I can feel you. I will adopt one soon for you."

On the day of a full moon in the evening around 5:40 pm, Gopika was sitting outside on a stone wall, did her first "Fortunate – Vomiting" after several prayers, the couple was blessed with a baby boy on 29th March 1930.

They gave the name of their first and only child, "Krishna." They were on cloud nine as they couldn't describe their euphoria in words. However, they were afraid and wanted to save their son from evil eyes. As being well-off in the village, everyone cast eyes on their wealth. The couple was in a huge dilemma, "How to keep their son protected?" A few weeks later, a fair was held in the village. Gopika went there to buy something for her little new one. After reaching the fair, she saw one small girl selling baby girl's costumes and accessories. One tricky idea emerged in her brain that she would buy all these for her little one Krishna, even though it sounds weird, but she smartly bought it.

Gopika came home and showed her shopping to Nand and said, "Hey!! look, what I bought for our gem-alike adorable son Krishna?"

"I can see with my both open eyes that you did the wrong shopping."

"Yeah, that's the point. This is the ONLY right choice for our son, as of now."

"I am still not getting you," He was confused.

"Listen, we will keep our son as a baby girl for a short time, just to protect our Krishna from evil eyes."

"Yeah, but why a baby girl? both are equal, isn't it?"

"Of Course! It is equal but for people like us, not for those who have a backward mindset. It is more than equal to us, as you know I always wanted to have a girl. Girls resemble Maa Durga. Hence Maa Durga will protect us from evil eyes."

In conservative territory, people are orthodox, not fully aware of anything and uneducated; therefore, they believe a girl has to leave her home after her marriage. She has no right to remain on her parental property afterwards. By this mindset, they would get no reason to envy our precious child.

They took advantage of people's backward mindset. They dressed up their son as a baby girl proudly for many years. The couple even gets Krishna's piercing done. This is another traditional culture also that every girl in the village has to get the piercing done in their childhood itself. Krishna's nose & ears were pierced. Just to strongly make people believe that they have given birth to a girl child. *(Somewhere, Gopika and Nand weren't happy with this selfish act. But they had left with no other choice to protect Krishna).*

"I want Krishna raised like a prince. I want to give better education to Krishna. Can we please relocate?"

"We will, Gopika."

The old couple wanted to give a good upbringing to their son. They thought for how long they would be able to hide Krishna from everyone? This is ethically not right as well to lie, and when Krishna would grow up, everyone would eventually come to know about it. They might harm him. Instead of revealing the truth to everyone in the village, they shifted to the nearest town called Ramgarh.

Chapter 6

A Fusion

On 25th December 1935, The couple reached Ramgarh without any pre-planning, i.e. where they would live, what they would eat, what would they do for a living etc. Ramgarh was not just a town; it was like heaven on the earth.

Serene lakes and temples surrounded Ramgarh. Everyone in the town was wearing modern clothes. And they had their private vehicles, bicycles, and good public transportation, but the polluted environment."

"What should I do here to live? As living costs in the town are expensive. How would I survive with my wife and son! To bear the urban expenses, I will have to work hard," He whispered.

"Where is Krishna?" Gopika asked,

"He was with you only."

"No, he was with you."

"Where is my son Krishna?" She looked in all directions and screamed.

Unexpectedly, a female voice came. She was nearly around nineteen years old, "Is this your son, Krishna?"

"Yes, Yes" Gopika ran towards the woman and grabbed Krishna in her arms.

"I am Ashima. Are you new here?"

"Yes, looking for a house to live in."

"Your Krishna mistakenly entered the house. I think destiny wants you to live with us as a tenant."

"Are you sure?"

"Yes, uncle, of course. Make yourself comfortable."

They got 1BHK on the ground floor. The couple got a shelter to live in, but that night Nand, couldn't sleep. He kept staring at his hand-made turban. He loved his traditional culture, so he used to wear a turban made with cotton fabric. He thought, in the town, everyone wears western clothes, and they require traditional dress occasionally. I can make a turban. I will give it a new trendsetting and sell it, will design it. The urban youth will attract to it and wear it. A new trend will call, 'Fusion'. People buy them for weddings and other occasions as well. I know, will be a unique concept for all. The way I would earn money. I will survive with my wife and son in the town. I will be able to send Krishna to a better school as well.

The next day, He shared this idea with his wife, Gopika. His wife respects his every decision, so she agreed without any further arguments. Nand made a long list of his new small venture's requirements for headwear. He needed a good place, pearls, decorative accessories, ancient royal badges, feathers, fabric like Rubia voile, F74 cloth, and a sewing machine on top priority. Somehow he arranged everything. He had learned its skill professionally to sell all types of traditional turban that people can wear in everyday lives, customising it with western clothes. He gave a new and unique trend.

Nand started getting a good amount of money by selling handmade headwear in the town. He bought his new small house & sent his son for better schooling. His son Krishna was a brilliant student and was leading his school's hockey team.

29th March 1948. A blessed day for the entire family. It was a day for Krishna's Birthday, and the couple held puja (a ritualistic act) at their home to celebrate their son's birthday. They didn't believe in the ceremony of blowing candles and cutting the cake on birthdays. They wanted to celebrate it traditionally. Hence, they held a puja ceremony at their home only.

Nand and Krishna wore cotton kurta-pyjama, Gopika wore an orange saree to impress her husband as the orange colour was Nand's favourite. They never had any arguments or conflicts other than playing a trick on each other. They were compatible. Gopika and Nand were a match made in heaven.

After worshipping God, they distributed blessed food, cotton candy and donated clothes to needy kids on the streets. The couple preferred to celebrate Krishna's birthday in this way only.

Krishna was fully grown up now and had completed his schooling. He was a bit concerned to get himself busy with some creativity. He never made any new friends from his neighbourhood. His friends were spoiling themselves into partying, clubbing etc. Krishna neither hated his friends nor liked their company.

Krishna wanted to help his father instead of ruining his adolescent age. However, Nand wanted to give his son a comfortable & easeful life.

He never wanted his son to struggle and do hard work, not even with him. As per Nand, Krishna was a silver spoon.

Chapter 7

Bizarre

*O*n 30th June 1949, one former King named Aditya Singh, 6" ft tall, healthy, and fit like a muscular man, dark-skinned, from the nearest village, visited the market & didn't find anything attractive to buy in the market. He saw one guy was selling designer handmade Turban.

It was attractive and unique. His eyes fell upon a glass box lying underneath the table. It had one unique designer turban.

He walked towards him & asked the price for one unique designer turban, "Well, creativity & art is priceless, it has no cost. However, how much does that boxed turban cost?"

"You are asking for that turban?" Nand pointed his finger towards a turban lying in a glass box underneath the table, tagged with the name 'Bizarre.'

"Yes, yes…that one," Mr Singh answered in eagerness.

"No sir, that box one is not for selling purposes. You can buy the other one. I am selling each for 15/- but I can negotiate."

King laughed out loud, "I believe you are new here. Don't you know me? My time is money, so make a deal as quickly as possible without turning away. How much for that turban?"

"Sir, whatever you are, I respect you from the bottom of my heart. However, "Bizarre" isn't for sale at all at any cost or conditions."

"Bizarre? Quite impressive, but why have you not been selling it? You can become one of the wealthiest men in the town. I can give you whatever price you offer me to sell it."

"Sir, you are wasting your time. I mention it's not possible, at any cost."

"What's holding you back?" Mr Singh asked.

"I never even let my wife know about this. If you are insisting on me, I would love to tell you. The turban is for my son. As you said, creativity and art are priceless. So much affection and sentiments for my only son, I can never substantiate, in exchange for money. This is my love for my son. I specially designed it for my son only. It almost took one year to get ready. I outsourced its material goods, which took a year. Another year to get its designing process done. As you can observe, this is not just an ordinary turban, an entirely royal crown. And I know everyone would like it as this is solely made with emotions and love for my son. I can't sell it. I do apologise."

Mr Singh was overwhelmed by his unconditional love towards his son.

"Where do you live?"

"I live two km from here, with my wife, Gopika and a son."

"What's the name of your son?"

"His name is Krishna."

"That's a nice name. Do you mind if I want to meet your family? If you like to come to my palace. I am inviting you for dinner along with your family. Don't forget to come with your son Krishna."

"I would love to. Surely, I will come. Thanks for the invitation," Nand replied to him with his warm gestures.

Nand reached his home in the evening, poured the whole day's story out to Gopika and son Krishna, that he met former King Mr Aditya Singh and how he got impressed and invited all of them to his residence.

"We have got a dinner invitation from the former King's palace. So be ready tomorrow."

"That's great. I can't believe it," Gopika said.

Krishna, "Congratulations, Baba, you are getting popular day by day," They all laughed, seeing each other and had dinner together. One hour later, they all went to sleep.

The next day early in the morning, Nand went for his work, and in the evening, they all got ready to go to King's house. Nand wore traditional wear: white kurta, dhoti along with red turban, 6 ft. tall, dark skin, wrinkles under eyes and on the forehead, bald and nearly obese, he looked old yet energetic. Gopika wore a red bling saree with a matching golden glitter blouse and put a red bindi on her forehead. Nand liked kajal in Gopika's eyes, so she put some kajal in her eyes. She had half black and grey hair. Still, she was looking as pretty as Nand saw her first time at their wedding ceremony. She was obese, energetic, fierce and brave. She had one black coloured small birthmark on her chin, which added beauty to her personality. Krishna liked the white colour. Hence, he chose white simple khadi fabric made kurta pyjama.

They all were in seventh heaven. They visualized while heading towards the former King's palace, on their way in a horse cart, that King would be living in a giant fancy bungalow decorated with expensive carpet and chandelier. The number of expensive vintage cars in the parking. And so many servants.

When they arrived at the King house, it was simply like a family. A small but neat and cleaned house with three rooms and one kitchen surrounded by mango trees. They knocked on the door, and one man, aged nearly, 70 years old, wearing a white dhoti and simple white kurta, came to open the door. Mr Singh and his wife were waiting for the guest. Mrs Sayukta Devi looked radiant, charming Queen, five ft. seven inches tall, wearing magenta pink coloured Rajasthani Bandhani (traditionally printed) chiffon saree. They all were already waiting at the dining table. Six seaters antique, ancient, wooden dining table grabbed Nand's attention.

Nand, Gopika and Krishna took their places one by one at the dining table. Despite being at King's house and sitting among influential people, Nand observed that Mr Singh's house and its entire environment was tranquil. He felt like they were at their own home instead of a King's palace. Living in a democratic country, ruling by Govt, Mr Singh and his entire family availed a simple life instead of a fancy king lifestyle.

The Cook Ramu interrupted their conversation by serving them food. Ramu served them puri (Bread), mixed vegetables, lentil soup, Matar paneer (made with soft Indian cottage cheese & peas) and Rice pudding (dessert) in exquisite glassware crockery. Nand & family enjoyed the meal wholeheartedly. Krishna was nervous and shy among all elders. He liked his comfortable life and being at his home only.

"Krishna, what do you do?" Mr Singh asked.

"I look after my parents. *(a polite way to say staying home and doing nothing much as of now)*. Sir! The fact is I recently completed my schooling. I want to help my father to sell turbans. That's it,"

A nineteen years old, Krishna was hesitant while interacting with affluent people as he had never been outside like this. Meanwhile, in between their conversation, Krishna randomly glanced at the fence of stairs. One girl of the same age group as Krishna, wearing a pink and white floral satin night suit, with a cute bow tie headband on her brown, shoulder-length, shiny and silky hair. She was staring at him without blinking. She passed him a killer smile and then went back into her room.

Nand and Gopika asked Mr Singh about his family.

"We have one son living in the USA. However, we always wanted to have one girl; hence we adopted a baby girl name Shelly Kumari," Mr Singh replied.

"And don't forget to introduce our Buzo. We have one more kid named Buzo," Mrs Sayukta Devi interrupted.

"Oh yes, we forgot to introduce my another, yet loyal one, Buzo; he is a German shepherd. I love Buzo more than my son. I am sorry, Rubal."

"Rubal?"

"Yes, my son, Rubal, lives in the USA."

"Oh, that's great."

"Yeah, but we have Buzo here. Say hello to Nand uncle and Gopika aunt." Mr Singh was trying to introduce Nand and his family to Buzo.

Nand was afraid of pets. So, he avoided playing with Buzo. He just gave it the cold shoulder.

"Alright! Gopika, we should head out."

"Yes, we are getting late."

"How was the food?" Cook Ramu asked.

"The food was mouth-watering, delicious food, I must say. No exaggeration if I would say I have never experienced such yum food until now. What a taste it was! I am self – inviting myself to visit your home once again for dinner, or we are taking Ramu along with us," Nand said jokingly.

"Yeah, all yours. Make yourself comfortable. It's your own house. You can come here whenever you want to come." Mr Singh responded.

Gopika looked at Nand, "Until now?! Are you sure you never had delicious food before?"

"Yeah, I mean the spices and ingredients used in all dishes; they all made its taste more delicious." Nand defended cook Ramu.

"I was just kidding," Gopika said.

Nand to Gopika, "I know you were kidding."

Nand to Mr Singh and his family, "Well, I am grateful for your kind and warm gesture to my family. We are ordinary people, yet, you made us feel at home and comfortable. Your entire family made our evening. I am grateful."

Nand and Gopika invited Mr Singh and his entire family to give them a chance to express their gratitude in a well-mannered way and to reciprocate their warm hospitality. They all finished their conversation, and they took their leave for home. It was one of the best days for Nand, Gopika and of course for Krishna.

The dark in the night around 2:00 am. Krishna was lying on the wooden bed at the terrace under the sky. In the bright moonlight, he was gazing at the stars and moon in the sky. Krishna was thinking about that girl, he couldn't forget the girl at King's house the way she was staring and smiling at him, it made him curious to know about her, and he wanted to meet and talk to her. The next day, Nand and Gopika got back to their routine work; Krishna, too, got busy finding a working path for himself. He was confused about his career.

Chapter 8

An offering

On 07th July'1949, around 8:00 pm, Nand reached home from his work. He heard voices of talking and laughter coming inside from his house. He entered curiously and saw Mr Singh with his whole family, wife Sayukta Devi, son Rubal from the USA, and daughter. Nand kept his turban filled bag aside at the corner and joined them in their conversation as well.

They all had dinner together. Gopika prepared simple vegetarian food: Veg Biryani (Rice dish), with Yoghurt & rice pudding (dessert), served to the King family. After dinner, in between their prolonged conversation, Gopika served them veg fritters with funnel cakes.

They all were sitting on the floor covered with a simple red velvet carpet. King's family was so grounded and kind-hearted. They were the true definition of being gentle and humble. Gopika moved towards the kitchen and started doing chores like cleaning and dishwashing. Krishna came inside the kitchen.

"Maa, I want to talk to you," Krishna distracted his mother, standing at the door.

"Yeah, son, what's the matter?"Gopika smiled and replied.

"I like that girl who has come along with Mr Singh and his family."

She was slightly busy. She overheard Krishna's word.

"Okay, (pause for one minute), What! You mean Shelly!? Daughter of Mr Singh! Shelly!?"

"Yes, Maa, Shelly. I never had such feelings before. Maa, the way she looks and smiles at me, it made me want to know and to think more about her." Krishna broke all the silence.

Gopika was stunned for a while, as she couldn't understand what to answer him. She looked at her son. She smiled and replied positively, "Both of you are too young for marriage. Son, I do understand your sentiments yet, our family backgrounds and cultures are different. What you want is not possible. And it will embarrass me if I talk to anyone about this. However, I will talk to your father first. If he agrees, we will talk further to Mr Singh," seeing her son upset, she tried her best to convince him. Meanwhile, a mother-son conversation, heard by Mrs Sayukta Devi. She interfered with all this and said," Krishna, my son, you and Shelly are juvenile. You have got a sight to choose right or wrong. An excellent desire as I can say that my daughter is talented, as pretty as a painting and brilliant. However, she is too adolescent and naive to think about marriage. We can't force her. Let Mr Singh be involved in it and get his reaction."

"What's going on here? What's the matter?" Mr Singh interfered surprisingly.

"Krishna, Nand's son, wants to get married to our daughter Shelly," Mrs Sayukta Devi poured everything into Mr Singh. Mr Singh was astonished for a while. Somehow, he managed to say, "This is impossible, Krishna! It is irrational. You do nothing. You just completed your schooling and looking after your parents only. You have no career right now. How can you even think like it, Krishna? You are a nice person. You belong to an honest, simple family. Yet this is not possible. We can't make your wish feasible." This unexpected bouncer ball irked him.

"I have immense respect for you and your entire family. I never interacted with her. I don't have wrong intentions for your daughter, but I know that I like her. I heard that every problem has a solution. We need to discover it. I will do anything for Shelly. I know we both are teenagers and underachievers, however, we won't stay the same. After five-six years, life won't be equivalent to as I am living today. All I want is a chance for Shelly."

"Listen, son, whatever it is! I can't go beyond my daughter's choice. Let me ask my daughter as well." He Looked at Shelly, "What do you want, Shelly? What do you think about Krishna?"

Shelly looked back at her father and said, "Paa, I too like Krishna. However, I do want to complete my further education first. I will marry him on one condition if he achieves great professional success on his own. It's not impossible, and I know it will take a few years only, but I will wait for him."

Everyone looked at Krishna to see his reaction; he smiled, bowed down, and said, "I will do anything for Shelly."

Both family members smiled, hugged each other, and gave them blessings. Shelly and Krishna saw each other, and they both were blushing. Mr Singh returned to his home late in the evening along with his family. After reaching home, Sayukta Devi prepared tea for her family. While serving tea to Mr Singh, she noticed his eyes were full of tears thinking his daughter will go to another house soon in a few years. They didn't observe earlier that their daughter had grown up so fast. She was near the age of her marriage. The couple got lost in flashback memories.

Chapter 9

An Adopted

1931, In March, nearby the Holi festival Mr Singh and Sayukta Devi went to an astrologer to know about the fortune of their kid as they believe in astrology. After reaching there, they noticed one girl, almost 1yr old, was crying continuously. When Sayukta Devi took her in arms, she stopped crying, started playing with her like they both knew each other for so long.

Sayukta Devi asked the astrologer about her mother. He said, "Her mother died after giving her birth, and I am the only one who looks after her."

She discussed with Mr Singh and said, "I want to adopt this baby girl at any cost."

Mr Singh asked the same to the astrologer. He refused, "She is my only daughter, my wife's fraction. How can I give her to you?"

Mr Singh said, "A child always needs a Maa (Mother). What if she asks you about her mother? How would she be raised so well without her mother? Hence do us a little favour and accept our wish. We assure you, we would never let her cry ever. She is our daughter from today onwards. And she would be raised like a princess."

The astrologer agreed to see a better lifestyle and good fortune for his daughter. Sayukta Devi took the baby girl in her arms, smiled and said, she is my Shelly.

On 08th July'1949 (12:30 am, India).

Telephone rang. Rubal picked up the phone.

"Hello…(a few minutes later), "No, I can't come immediately, I have to extend my leaves, please try to understand," He disconnected the call in aggression.

"Hey, Rubal! What happened, son!?"

"Nothing Mama, I just got a call from my office. They don't want to extend my leave. I don't want to go to the USA, Maa. I want to stay home for some more time."

"If there is some urgent work call, then you can head to the USA. Paa and I will manage everything here. Work is worship. It's not acceptable if you take it so casually. Rubal, you can move back to the USA," Mrs Sayukta Devi ordered him.

"I arrived in India a few days back only. We didn't spend enough time together. Now I will have to go back again. So, I thought of extending my leaves to spend more time with you and Paa. I will get my packing done and book tickets by tomorrow, if you insist."

At Nand's home, Krishna asked his father, "Baba, what path should I choose to work with professionally?"

"My son, do whatever you want to do. Just do it with all your heart."

"Baba, I have never been so ambitious, hence never thought to do anything other than helping you in turban selling. But if I have to choose something professionally now,

I am thinking about one incident, do you remember? When we used to live in the village, I have some blurry memories of that time. Maa got sick for almost one week, and there was no doctor available to take care of her and no clinics, chemist shops at all. Now, I got to know the value of doctors. Hence, I want to be a doctor so that I can always be available for you and Maa."

"That's my boy. I wish you luck. God bless you."

Krishna visited the nearest medical college and enquired about its entrance examination and all other formalities. He got admission to a medical college. He started living in a college hostel to remain solely focused on his studies.

Krishna was an earnest student in college. He was good at his studies. He studied wholeheartedly and got his M.B.B.S. degree successfully with the highest grades.

Chapter 10

A Quietus

On 23rd June 1955, Nand and Gopika decorated their house like the Diwali festival.

Nand purchased an orange colour cruiser bike to give to his son on his special day. The orange colour was Nand's favourite.

That day, Nand was ecstatic. He was, again and again, saying to Gopika, "My son is arriving with his degree. With his MBBS degree. Now I can die in peace. I don't have regrets in my life. I lived my life fully." He was dancing and bouncing around, "My son is a doctor. I became the father of a doctor. I can leave the world peacefully."

Gopika looked at him in aggression. She wanted to say something, their house's doorbell rang.

"Maa….Baba….please open the door," He screamed, outside standing at the door.

"Krishna. Our son has arrived. Wait a sec. I am going to open the door."

"Let me open the door the last time for my son."

"The Last time!? *whispered* Gopika was taken aback by his words, then she ignored them. Their son had arrived home. Nand and Gopika welcomed their son, Krishna.

"I will show you my degree, but first, promise me something."

"What promise?" Both asked.

"After seeing my medical degree, you both have to give me my favourite gift."

"Okay!! We will give you whatever you want," Nand responded.

He handed over his medical degree in Nand's hand. Nand put on his glasses to see the medical degree and emotionally said while showing it to Gopika, "Our baby …our Krishna, has now become Dr Krishna. We are proud parents of a Doctor. Gopika, our son will be there to look after you when I am gone; now I can die in peace."

"I have been observing you since morning. Please stop talking rubbish. Today is our son's day, a blessed day. Would you please not behave and talk like this? We all need you always. So, what if our son has become a doctor? It's our time to live more, to live at home and spend quality time together. It's your retirement time from work."

"Yes, it's my retirement time. I can die in peace. You are right."

"You started it again. Retirement means staying home and enjoying life with family instead of going to work every day. Now our son will be earning for us," Gopika said aggressively.

Nand kept staring at her and smiling, "Love you, Gopika."

Krishna interrupted, "If your romantic time is over, will you please look at your son and give him gifts?"

"What gifts do you want, my son? Just tell your Baba".

"Oh Maa – Baba, I missed you so much, especially home-cooked food, Maa. I got bored with eating the same hostel food every day. They don't even maintain their food quality. They focus only on their quantity. You don't have any clue how much I was missing your homemade food, my favourite food, delicious and mouth-watering. I am malnourished Maa, what would you cook for me today?" Krishna asked.

"I know what you like eating when you are damn hungry. I know your favourite dish, Krishna. I already prepared your favourite: *Rice Pudding (dessert), Red Kidney Beans and Rice*. Here you go, Dr Krishna." Gopika smiled at his son, and she served him a big platter of his favourite dish."

"And Baba, What about you? How would you show your love to me?"

"I have got a bike for you. Your favourite Bike."

'In black colour?"

"No, it's my favourite colour."

"No way, Baba! Please, I want black, Maa. I knew he would take revenge on his son because I was staying away from him for such a long period."

"I know your favourite colour. But I want to give you my favourite to give you a lifetime blessing, not for any revenge. You will understand soon why orange is the colour." Nand responded.

Nand got emotional, and he left to his room without eating anything.

"Baba, I am sorry. I know it's your blessings and love towards me. I was kidding. Are you mad at me?" Krishna spoke in a loud tone behind his back.

"I am not mad at you, son. I want peace," Nand responded while heading towards his room.

"Peace!? Baba, what's wrong with you? Why are you talking to me like this?" Krishna asked.

"I love you and Gopika more than my life. I left a purple box inside your closet. It's my blessings for your auspicious day. Now I want some rest," Nand replied.

47

"Maa, what's wrong with Baba? Why is he behaving like a stranger. I came home after a long time, and he left without eating anything. I was expecting him to have dinner together. He was proud when I handed over my degree in his hand, yet, why is he behaving rudely now. His behaviour is strange to us. Did you notice?" Krishna asked.

"He must be feeling tired. Did you pay attention that he just said he wants to sleep? So, he is just tired, nothing serious," She was trying to convince his son and herself that everything was normal.

"Maa, are you hiding something?"

"No, you want *Rice? Rajma? Anything?*" She was trying to divert her mind.

"Are you sure everything is fine? Did you notice his weird behaviour?"

"Don't think too much. Nothing is wrong with Baba, now would you please stop overthinking? Have your dinner and go to sleep in your room."

"No, I will sleep with Baba in his room tonight. I want to talk to him. I have a bunch of matters to discuss and share. We both son and father will keep talking overnight."

"I understand your feelings. Everything is fine. All is well. Your Baba is fine. We will all have breakfast tomorrow. You can talk to him at the breakfast table." Gopika said in her melancholy voice as if she was hiding something.

She was hiding a mishap, few ill-fated indications since morning. While cleaning dishes, her bangle got broken in the morning, and a tiny box filled with vermilion fell all over the ground while cleaning the house. She didn't want to recall it. In Indian tradition, both are a considerably bad omen.

Gopika was unable to sleep, got up early at 4 am. She went to Nand's room. What she saw was dismal. She screamed like hell. She was calling her son, "Krishna, please come to my room."

She rushed to Krishna's room. "Krishna!.......my son! Please get up, your Baba.. look at your Baba once."

"Wh...at! What happened to Baba?" He got up hurriedly.

"He fainted in his restroom, is lying on the floor."

As Krishna heard about his Baba, he had no courage to go to his Baba's room as he was in excruciating pain. He called the ambulance immediately and took his father to the nearest hospital.

At the hospital, while interacting with the doctor.

"One person can come along inside to be with the patient." The doctor to Gopika.

"Yes, my son will come along with you."

"No, Maa. Never, I want to go, but I can't see my father, unconscious. I wanted him at the breakfast table this morning. Not in the hospital. Maa, let me just be at peace. Get off my back. I told you to let me stay with Baba last night. I wanted to talk to him. You can go. I won't be able to go inside in cardiology, where Baba got admitted. Get your act together." He lost his temper.

Even Gopika couldn't understand what happened to Nand. She felt helpless when she saw him lying on the ground. She can't imagine her life without Nand. "I can't even think of living without Krishna's father. I shouldn't think like this. He is fine." She whispered.

Krishna and Gopika were looking strangely at each other. They both couldn't understand what happened to Nand.

"Doctor, please save my father. He is my entire world," Krishna clasped his hands, requesting the doctor.

"We are trying our best, Krishna," the Doctor consoled.

The doctor moved inside and came after 10 minutes...

"How's my father? Is he conscious now? Can we meet him? Did he call my name?" To looking at his mother, "Maa, let's go to Baba, now he is fine, he must be waiting for you and me. Come on, let's go inside to see him."

"I am sorry, Krishna, please try to control yourself. Mr Nand is no more. We couldn't save him. Krishna, we are sorry."

"What do you mean by sorry, doctor!" Krishna lost his temper, "Doctor, how's my father? He can't go without talking to me and taking his wife's permission. My father cannot go anywhere. It's his time to go to work, to sell his turban as he introduced 'Fusion' attire customized western with traditional. How smart! It's not his time to sleep. Please ask him to go to work. Please ask him to wake up. Please ask him that his little son Krishna is outside to meet him and help him with his work. Please ask him to get up once. Please, I want my father back," He screamed out loud, "Baba, please come back to your Krishna."

"Try to control yourself, Krishna. Now you have to look after your mother also."

Krishna's heart shattered into several pieces. The worst feeling ever for a son to see his father's death. To know that he would never meet that person ever again.

Shelly's family too arrived at the hospital. Mr Singh consoled Krishna and his mother. Their family and relatives performed Nand's last rituals.

In the evening, at almost 8 pm, Gopika was standing in front of Nand's photo frame covered with garlands, gazing at it. She started talking to Nand as if he was still alive, "You left me alone, all alone. On our son's most important day, the day of his wedding, you will not be with us. Moreover, I will have to wake up, prepare food, eat alone, do all my routine work. However, my life would never be the same again. You betrayed and left us alone. I will never forgive you for this," She wiped her tears and lost herself in nostalgia.

Krishna started living upset and depressed. The emptiness was ruining his intelligence. He used to come home late in the night. It had been almost fifteen days he didn't eat food. He was already depressed in shock of his father's sudden demise. He almost lost his senses. Krishna fell sick. He didn't know how to handle and get over this trauma.

Gopika noticed her son's condition. She was getting worried about his health. She lost her husband. She didn't want to lose her son at this age. He was an adult. He had a whole life ahead. He couldn't give up on everything like this.

Krishna came home by evening. And he was going to sleep.

"Death is a bitter truth. Everyone will depart from life after completing their purpose. Life's purpose," Gopika interrupted.

"I am sorry for my rude behaviour, but I don't know how to live without Baba. I don't know. I feel emptiness everywhere. I need help, help me." He left for his room to hide his tears and emotions.

Chapter 11

An Animal Cloud

*J*uly 1955, the year was sort of a curse for the family. But somehow good too as Krishna got his MBBS degree successfully. Gopika was getting worried seeing her son's condition. She decided to get him married soon. She visited Mr Singh the next day and asked him about Krishna and Shelly's marriage. Mr Singh remained silent for a second. Gopika couldn't understand his silence.

"What happened. Is everything okay?" Gopika asked.

"Yes ...everything is perfectly okay.....except that my daughter will leave us soon. She is my world. I request you, please look after and fulfil her all wishes," Mr Singh said.

"I promise. Shelly would come to my house as a daughter, not a daughter-in-law. Don't worry about it," Gopika replied.

Mr Singh and Mrs Sayukta Devi called their priest (Astrologer) to ask him the best day for their daughter's marriage.

Shelly came from her friend's house, and she gazed at her family in astonishment, all sitting together with Gopika Aunty.

She asked, "What's going on?"

"Oh! Gopika aunt, when did you come over? How are you?" she said, touching her feet... *(An Indian ritual of paying respect to elders).*

"Yes, all good. Practice calling me Maa instead of aunt."

Mr Singh interrupted, "You are getting married soon. We called the priest also to get an auspicious time and date for your and Krishna's marriage."

As Shelly got to know she will be getting married soon, she blushed and hugged her father.

"Oh... Paa, you are great. You kept your promise even after Nand uncle is no more. You are such a King Paa in all manners. You know the true value of commitments and words."

At Krishna's Home:

"Where have you been, Maa?" Krishna asked.

"I went to meet Mr Singh. I wanted to talk about the matter of your marriage."

"Please try to understand. I am not ready to marry yet."

"May I know the reason."

"Without Baba, I can't. I almost forgot how to smile."

"Yes, my son. I know that's why I want you to get married, to get your life back. Don't worry about me. I will be fine. You will get the company of my other child Shelly."

"Okay, Maa. I won't argue on this matter as you want good for me."

12th December 1955, on the day of their marriage. Gopika was as happy as she had taken Krishna for the first time in her arms. She couldn't describe her happiness in words. She put some little make-up on, a red bindi and kajal. Nand gave the words of honour that she would never abandon these things even after Nand left the world. As he would see her from heaven, he didn't want to see her without kajal and bindi. She wore white-coloured with bling artwork, party wear saree and red bling shawl crafted with fine wool.

She got it from Srinagar by Nand as he visited Kashmir for three weeks to examine different textiles and explore its market. Nand always wanted to be a great textile businessman. He tried his best to be one of them. After relocating to Ramgarh, he didn't get better opportunities to move into another new place for work purposes and enhance skill; therefore, he remained in his comfort zone.

"If he were here today, he would never have let me wear my favourite white colour. He would have given me an orange coloured or red bling saree. He was a diehard fan of these colours. I couldn't even think to go beyond his choices. Why did he leave me?" Gopika was looking aged with a wrinkled face, yet still so charming and glowing. Her inner beauty was reflecting on her face.

"Where is Krishna? He must be getting ready." She searched for him.

Krishna wore his father's pearl white sherwani, breeches trousers, silver velvet mojari Jutti. 5'9" tall, fair, Krishna looked like a perfect groom any girl could wish. He opened a purple box and wore "Bizarre – A Royal Crown" (lavender, red and orange coloured). A unique turban named Bizarre was specially designed by his father Nand for his wedding day.

Krishna, Gopika and a few guests reached the wedding venue in a car. After arriving at the wedding venue (Shelly's house), Mr Singh & family welcomed the guests. They asked Krishna to sit on a horse as if a prince came here to win the princess, riding on it. A ritual they had to perform. As far as it was a ritual, Krishna got agreed. As he sat on a horse named Baadal, he saw a butterfly and started running behind it to play with it. Krishna was a Doctor, not an equestrian.

He couldn't read horse language. Krishna was sitting on the horse & Baadal was running behind a butterfly to play with it. Everyone got scared, thinking Krishna would fall on the ground and might get wounded. One equestrian controlled Baadal. Krishna was out of danger. The whole situation mixed with joy and fear. The Joy: The way Baadal was running behind the butterfly and The Fear: Krishna was slightly in danger.

One group of small children standing among the crowd laughed at Krishna and the horse by seeing the whole situation. It was life-threatening. The group of witty children alleviated the level of stress, made everyone laugh.

Krishna entered Shelly's house and saw the same naïve girl staring at him standing at the fence when he came to this house for the first time. That teen girl was grown up completely and was wearing a yellow lehenga, green coloured blouse, red and yellow coloured saree. She wore bling red bangles in her henna painted hands. 5'2" Shelly Kumari was looking like a doll, completely Krishna's princess.

In the evening, around 9 pm. Mr Singh and Mrs Sayukta Devi gave their daughter's hand to Krishna. *"She is all yours, but never leave her as she has never lived alone."* The couple tied in a blessed knot, exchanged garlands, and took blessings from their elder ones as per the ritual.

Mr Singh gifted Krishna one of his favourite vintage cars fully decorated with pink and red roses. Mr Singh and the family broke down while performing the Bidai ritual for their daughter.

Krishna and Shelly reached home, a home where Krishna was living with his Maa. They took Nand's blessings by touching Baba's photo.

"Congratulations, son, your life's new journey has started; make it worth living."

"Thanks Maa but I miss Baba."

"I know, but we both are helpless. Go to your room. I won't hold you back. Your life partner Shelly must be waiting for you."

Krishna touched Gopika's feet to take her blessings. He was a bit nervous and scared about that Baadal incident.

Gopika could easily see her son's nervousness. "He is still like my innocent baby," she whispered.

Krishna headed towards his room. In the room, Krishna and Shelly spoke to each other for the first time. Krishna asked Shelly, "You are a princess, you were living in a big house, then why did you choose me? I live in a simple house."

"I appreciate your simplicity, that's it."

"Okay"

"You are phenomenal and hunky. I am shorter than you; why did you choose me?"

"I love the way you look at me," He answered.

Perfection is a myth. When two imperfect souls meet, they make perfect bonding in a relationship.

Krishna was a single earner in his family. He was facing challenges and obstacles in his professional life. Krishna believed that there are no shortcuts to be wealthy and successful in life except hard work & focus. Krishna did his best and bought a big house for his mother and wife, Shelly.

Chapter 12

A Little Fairy

*I*n July, the couple was blessed with a baby girl. As she was born in the rainy season, they named their daughter Barkha. She had charming features, a beautiful glowing pinkish skin tone and black eyes. Krishna used to spend most of the time in his clinic. Shelly used to remain busy with her household chores. Hence Barkha got closer to Gopika more than her parents. Gopika used to tell her granddaughter fairy tales.

Years have passed, Barkha was now a five years old child. Krishna gave her daughter a gift.

Krishna wrote a small note for his daughter with golden ink: *"Writing To my daughter on her 5th birthday,14th July 1971 (Wednesday). Barkha – a lovely baby girl child, she changed my life from ugly sides. A fortunate girl. Be blessed forever, my doll. - Daddy.*

Barkha listens to fairy tales from her grandmother, the way she used to sleep.

Gopika started telling her a story, "On the moon, a Lil fairy used to live with her family, and one day she wanted to visit earth. She wanted to see how people on earth live."

From the moon, she used to look down at the earth.

"What sort of those lights are?" she asked her father.

"That's earth. People without wings live there. They are not like us. Their lifestyle is different," her father said.

"I want to go to earth to see how people live there. Please allow me. I will come back surely. I will be safe and secure by myself," she insisted.

"Not in the slightest. You are a fragile and attractive Lil fairy. You won't be safe on earth. People will kill you," Her father refused her to go there.

Lil fairy stopped eating food and stopped talking to her father.

"I wanna go. My friends have also been there on earth in the dark. They returned safely."

"They are lying. Your friends are just making up stories," father was trying to convince her.

"I know they are not. They all went to earth last night. And they will again go tomorrow using their wings. I, too, wanna go," she requested.

"Maybe they were not lying, but being a protective father, I don't want to let you misuse your wings. Our wings are blessed and divine. We have these, but not to fly around. We should be grateful that we got divine power.

And you, my Lil fairy, are more blessed than all your fairy friends. Just look at your beauty and wings. You have got pink colour wings. We call you Lil fairy to make you different. Even if you don't know about yourself how beautiful you are, my Lil fairy. You are so different and charming," her father said.

Lil Fairy got upset. She didn't look beautiful when she gets upset. Seeing Lil fairy sad, her father allowed her to go to the Earth.

"You can go to explore the Earth, yet I want one promise," her father said.

"Promise? What sort of promise?"

"Promise me that you won't go to a crowded place. And don't let any human touch your wings. If any human touches your wings, it will become stronger. You will get cursed that your divine soul won't go to heaven after death. And you will get a chance to be born like a human on the earth. I don't want that. You can only go to the dark forest area. Not anywhere else. I know you would return to us, yet if for some reason you can't come back to the moon, try to burn your wings by using sunlight and don't tell anyone that you are a Lil fairy. Don't let your wings get misused by people living on the earth. Your wings are powerful and divine."

"No, I would come back to you. I won't break your trust. Don't make me vulnerable," the Lil fairy said.

The next night, she left the moon with her friends to see the earth. She has arrived, in the dark forest, she was mesmerized, could only say, "WOW! This planet is so beautiful."

She requested her one fairy friend take her to the mountains, the Crowded place and the Riverbank.

No, we can't go to the Riverbank. People living near the Riverbank might harm us. I can show you the whole dark forest. And before sunrise, we will have to leave to protect our wings. I apologise." Her fairy friend replied.

"People living on earth can see the sunrise?" Lil fairy asked.

"Yes. We can't stay here for that, as we are already blessed. And the sun rays are so strong that our wings can burn. Hence we will have to leave as soon as possible."

While roaming in the dark forest, Lil fairy got lost. She lost her way and fairy friends. Her friend searched around for her, yet they couldn't find Lil fairy.

Her fairy friends flew back to the moon before sunrise.

Lil fairy reached the Riverbank, a dangerous zone for her because people on the earth were living there. She started crying. She was blessed with pink wings and pink tears.

One boy near the river came to drink water. He saw Lil Fairy, and he said amazed, "Who are you? Are you from a fancy dress competition? And lost your way home? Isn't it?"

"I don't know what you are saying. Please don't create a scene here and speak a little slowly. So that people living here can't listen to our conversation. I lost my way. Please take me to the Dark Forest."

"The Dark Forest? The Dark Forest is scary. Why do you want to go there?"

"Because I belong to Moon, I am a Lil Fairy".

The boy started laughing, "This is impossible. Wait a minute. Let me pinch myself. That's honest. You are so alluring like a beautiful painting. Trust me." And he bent down on his knees - "Will you marry me?"

Lil fairy could only say in her fearful voice, "Daa…dark forest….please…I want to go to the Dark Forest. I am feeling nervous here. I don't know, I am afraid, please don't talk about this to anyone, promise me. I have to leave before sunrise, as my father must be waiting for me. I promised him."

"Okay, I will take you to the Dark Forest."

That boy agreed to take her to the dark forest. The fairy felt that the boy was nice by heart. She asked, "How much time was left for the sun to rise?"

"Almost one and a half hours," The boy replied.

"What's your name?" She asked.

"This is Joe."

"Joe, can you show me around? The mountains? The place where people live? I came here to see and explore everything."

"Sure," Joe said.

"Yet do promise me that before the sunrise, you would allow me to go to my home, where my father and fairy friends live," Lil fairy said.

"Hey!! I do promise that I will let you go. By the way, what's your name?" Joe asked.

"I already told you. Just Lil Fairy, only," She said.

"Oh! Yeah. I want one promise from you that you would let me touch your wings?" he asked.

She didn't reply. *Smiled*

The boy took her along with him and started showing her around the mountains, the Riverbank, standing from miles away, the boy showed his house to the Lil fairy.

"Lil fairy, look at there. That's my house."

"That's so fantastic. Can you take me there to your house?"

"No, that's not possible. It's okay for me but not for you. You are from a different world and so beautiful. You would be caught easily by people. They can harm your beauty and wings."

"Am I beautiful?"

"Yes. You are so beautiful it's like I am watching a beautiful dream that I never wanna wake up from."

Lil fairy and Joe became good friends, like they have known each other since birth. Joe kept watching the time. Just fifteen minutes left for the sunrise. Boy didn't want to tell her the sunrise time, as he knew that she would be leaving soon.

"Joe, what are you hiding? What time is it? You promised me that you would allow me to go. Take me to the dark forest right now," She got scared.

"No, I won't take you to the dark forest. You would be living here forever with me," Joe said.

Lil fairy started crying.

"Hey, stop crying. I was kidding. You are the dumbest crying fairy. We are standing in the Dark Forest with ten

61

minutes left for the sunrise. You can leave for your home. Your father must be waiting for you," Joe said.

Lil fairy took his hand and let him touch her wings. She smiled and flew back to the moon before sunrise.

"Awesome, just awesome, this story was one of the best stories you ever told," Barkha cuddled her Granny and continued, "I wanna listen to a real story, promise me that someday you would tell me a real story."

"Yes. Promise."

And they both left to sleep.

Chapter 13

Mother Nature

On 15th April 1979, Gopika told Barkha a real story. "Many years ago, when your father was young, your grandpa and I used to live in the village. We had a small house there. We shifted in the town because we wanted to give a better upbringing to your father. And since we were living in the town. We have never visited the village."

Barkha curiously looked at Gopika, "Wow! I want to see our other house in the village."

"For sure, I will take you, my child."

"No, Grandma. I want to go as soon as possible." She was curious to see the beauty of the village.

"Now isn't possible. I will talk to your Daddy in the morning, will make the plan, you can go to sleep, Gunnnnnnnight love."

"Alright, but plan as soon as possible, Gunnnnnnnight."

The next morning, at the breakfast table, Gopika discussed Barkha's wish with Krishna. Krishna was working as a senior surgeon. However, he was still an obedient child for his mother. Hence, without indulging in an unnecessary argument, he agreed and said, "Maa, whenever you want to go, I will arrange your travel to the village, and you can take Barkha along with you, but you would travel with our driver."

On 19th April 1979, Gopika and Barkha visited the village in their car and entered their house, which was closed for many years. The house was full of dust and spider webs. It looked not less than a scary haunted house. Their other nest, a treehouse, where Gopika lived for many years with her beloved Nand, was destroyed by people living in the village. How cruel!

'Before entering the house, as of now, need to get it cleaned first.'

They had already arrived in the village. Gopika didn't want to let go of her Granddaughter's curiosity. 'I have something special to demonstrate to you. But I want one promise that you would follow my instructions.'

'I promise, Grandma.'

Gopika was in her wheelchair, a foldable wheelchair. After Nand's demise. Barkha gave her a reason to live. She tied a blindfold on Barkha's eyes, held her hand, and asked her to follow directions. She reached the destination and removed the blindfold from Barkha's eyes. She contemplated, scanning everything like her eyes lenses have binoculars. She witnessed the beauty of nature.

She stared at acres of land, trees, roses, and plantation, a river with crystal clear water. She was able to see nature's reflection in the river. She felt her feet at heaven on the earth.

She kept staring at the village's beauty without blinking. Barkha wanted to speak a lot but managed to say, "Is this ours?"

"Yes, my darling, mother nature is for all."

"Grandma, how can we make mother nature love us?"

"We need to keep mother nature protected from dust, plastic, pollution, and then mother nature loves you back with health and oxygen."

"Why we have been living in a crowded and polluted town? Can we shift here?"

"We will come here often if you wish. But shifting here is not possible. My darling, this is your growing age, you are a young girl, being your elder, our responsibility to give you a better education, we can't shift here. Where would you study? There is no school and higher education. What about Krishna & Shelly? I mean your parents, they live in the town, and we live in the village? How will it be possible? I need a word of honour that you will never discuss further on this matter of shifting here. We should get back home. We are getting late."

In the evening, around 7 pm, they both returned to their home. Krishna came on time for dinner.

"How was the village trip?"

"Just an experience Daddy, especially with Grandma. She is so energetic and still fit and fine. Not less than a miracle. I am so keen to shift there. My strict Grandma is not allowing me to do so." Then she put her eyeglasses on and started an act of Grandma, how her Grandma used to cough, sneeze, walk when she had extreme backache and how she disciplined Barkha for not doing things that her Grandma doesn't like. Seeing a little one's mimic, Krishna and Gopika both started laughing.

"What a joyful family it is! Touchwood," Shelly murmured while serving food to Krishna.

Chapter 14

A Misery

$\mathscr{I}$n the morning on 20th April 1979, at 05:30 am. It was raining heavily. The telephone rang rapidly at Krishna's home. It was the call of Dr Sharma. Dr Sharma and Dr Krishna were companions since college time. They studied and practiced medicine together. However, at the hospital, Dr Krishna was working in a senior position than Dr Sharma.

Dr Krishna received the call.

"Hello, what happened! Why did you call?" Dr Krishna asked.

"Sir, it's an emergency case. Sir, please reach the hospital. The patient has lost a lot of blood. I can't tell everything over the call. It's a police case," Dr Sharma said.

"What the hell? Police case, in our hospital? What are you saying, Dr Sharma?"

"Sir, I can't say everything over the call, please don't waste time and come straight to the hospital," Dr Sharma said.

Dr Krishna reached the hospital.

"Which emergency case got admitted this morning?" Dr Krishna asked at the reception.

"Room no. 205, Sir."

"Thank you, Ms Bina."

Dr Krishna proceeded to see the patient.

"Dr Sharma, where is the patient?"

"It's right over there, the fourth bed."

"What's the matter, the police case you were talking about over the call? What happened to him? What did he do?" Dr Krishna asked.

"Are you Dr Krishna?" Meanwhile, Mr Lal, the patient's father, interrupted their conversation. "He is psycho, I think... my son is psycho...Dr," Mr Lal said.

"Psycho! I am sorry your son got admitted. My colleague mentioned in the morning that he lost a lot of blood. He needs your concern, at least. Stop using such word about him as of now. Would you please act wisely? You are his father. He needs your support," Dr Krishna reprimanded.

"What should I say? My son Vineesh slit his wrists. He was going through misery. He was in an insane love affair for just six months only. He likes a girl and wants to marry her, notwithstanding that girl rejected him."

"Girl! Did you see that girl?" Dr Krishna asked.

"Yes, her name was Manika. I don't think it was her fault. However, she came to my house last week and insulted him because my son does nothing. He was dependent on my earnings, and he wants to inherit my wealth. Doctor, he was jobless, yet, he procrastinates everything. He doesn't even try to earn and make his life better. He doesn't even respect his parents. He is my son, yet he is good for nothing. Even I scolded him last week. He was suffering from depression, and in his misery, he cut his veins. Police officers also came in the morning to take our statements. After taking my son's statements, they gave doctors a green signal for his treatment."

"How old is he?"

"Doctor, my son, Vineesh is twenty-one years old."

"What a name!"

"He is my only son. Being his father, I have some expectations from him," Mr Lal started crying.

"Oh gosh!! I have no words. These youngsters can't tolerate and handle life's failure and rejections. I can't say too much about this matter. I would only say they put themselves and their parent's lives too into trouble with such ridiculous acts. I am sorry to say, yet they are just too weak to take such big steps without a second thought. What a coward. The way they think about escaping the world. They don't even think about their parents and their own life. Life is a gift, a precious one. Adolescence is an age of creating life, not destroying it. At some level, we all face failure and rejections in life. Every problem has a solution. Just share it with your close friends and family. Whatever you are going through, pour your heart out to them. All you need to take is just a single step to find someone to talk to and share who can listen to you. That's it. Being a doctor, I would suggest taking the counsellor's help, if you require it. I do understand life isn't an easy game. But we can't get so serious about everything. It can be easy if we handle it at our ease. Rejection isn't enough of a reason to give up on our beautiful lives. There are so many things to do to make parents proud. All youngsters should understand this. I want to meet him. I want to tell all this to your son," Dr Krishna said.

"Sir, he is sleeping and unconscious. As I told you over the phone, he lost lots of blood. We might not be able to save him," Dr Sharma intervened.

"Don't say this. We are doctors, and we can't lose hope without trying our best. We will try hard to save him."

And they both tried their best to treat twenty-one-year-old Vineesh, who was lying unconscious. His fifty-one years old father was standing outside his room and praying for his son's recovery.

In the Intensive Care Unit, doctors and nurses were looking determined to save the patient Vineesh. A tick-tock of the clock motivating them to try their best.

Dr Krishna was giving him oxygen through a nasal cannula to transfer breathing. Doctors kept pushing and pumping his chest to increase blood flow to his heart with machines.

A drop of sweat fell on scissors, distracting Krishna. He missed Barkha.

"What's the time?" Dr Krishna asked as he forgot his watch at home as he had to rush towards the hospital last morning after getting the emergency call.

"Sir. Its 21st April, 6:00 am. What happened? Are you alright?" Dr Sharma asked.

"Seriously! Oh ! Lord, This patient Vineesh didn't even let me see the time, for last day." *whispered* "Yeah, I miss my daughter Barkha. I know I am getting emotional and inappropriate to leave a patient in this condition, but my instincts disturb me and do not allow me to concentrate here. I want to see my daughter. You keep trying. As soon as he wakes up, or you see any improvement, call me. I will be back in 40 mins."

At Krishna's home around 06:15 am, Shelly prepared breakfast for Krishna, "You didn't come home last evening. Maa and Barkha were asking about you."

"How's my daughter?"

"She was waiting for you yesterday for dinner. But you didn' come so she slept without having dinner. She said she got tired. May be due to the village trip, day before yesterday. She is sleeping. We didn't disturb her," Shelly said.

"Okay, then. Let Barkha sleep. I came to see her once. I have to leave again."

"You just came minutes before, you haven't had a wink of sleep, and you are leaving again. What's the matter?" Shelly asked in a melancholy voice.

"Nothing, my love. One patient has been struggling between life and death. So this is why I have to leave early again. I won't be able to come home this evening either. Ask maa to not wait for me and don't make my dinner. I am getting a call from the hospital. I need to leave."

"Can you stay just five minutes more?"

He properly sanitized his hands, wiped his face with wet tissues, "You are the best wife. I do respect your efforts and patience. The way you are looking after our mother and daughter so nicely. I have no complaints. Yet, I am sorry that I do not give enough time at home for you and my daughter. You do understand it better, as this is my profession," he was emotional & continued…

"You know this patient Vineesh is a critical case. He is at a young age. His age is not to get admitted into the hospital and die."

"What happened to him, can I ask?"

"You are my better half. You can ask me whatever you want to ask. There is nothing to hide. However, I don't feel like talking about a numbskull, can say."

"Numbskull? That's not quite a word to use for a serious patient."

"Yeah, I know, he is an oaf. I don't like such a youngster."

"An Oaf? You never say anything wrong and discuss things like this at home about your patient, then what's wrong with this patient?"

"Nothing worth discussing. Leave. I will discuss this later. I have to leave now."

"I wish a speedy recovery to your patient. He will feel better soon. Don't worry."

He passed her a smile, kissed her forehead, "Bye, my love." He left for the hospital.

"Bye. Take Care…"

Krishna left swiftly without listening to her words. He was driving towards his hospital. He overlooked to see the speed of the car and was almost saved from an accident.

"What a beauty of life and miracle," he whispered. Dr Krishna reached the hospital as per his commitment in 40 minutes. Doctors are visible angel on the earth.

Shelly was feeling anxious since morning. She had a gut feeling that something unexpected was about to come. She was trying hard not to think like that, yet, she couldn't restrict herself.

Around 11:00 am Shelly, called her elder brother Rubal in the USA. She gave him the nickname Rubi to tease him. Shelly called him to ask about their family's health.

Mr Singh and Sayukta Devi had also shifted to the USA after Shelly's marriage. They both were living there with their son only. So she was getting worried about her parents and brother. She dialled The USA number…

"Hello, I am Shelly from India. Please transfer the call to Rubal."

"Hello, ma'am. Rubal Sir is not home," The maid answered the call.

"Where is my Paa? Can you please transfer my call to him?" *aggression*

"Yes, ma'am," Call transferred to Mr Singh.

"Hello, Paa! How are… ?" She started sobbing.

"What happened, my doll? Why are you crying?" Mr Singh asked.

"Paa, I don't know. I don't feel good. I'm feeling anxious and sad. How are you all?"

"We all are good here, don't get worried about all of us. We are all doing well here and perfectly fit as a fiddle. And your Rubi is also good," He laughed.

"Okay. Ask Rubi to call me back when he reaches home."

"Yeah, he comes late. Sometimes he stays in the office only. He is trying to start his own business. So he doesn't have much time for his family. He keeps himself busy at his work. You know that our lazy Rubi has become responsible and gentlemanly. Your Rubi is quite a workaholic," Mr Singh said.

"Okay, Paa, that's good. I was only worried about all of you. That's why I called. Nothing else."

"Well, how's my son-in-law Krishna and everyone at home?" He asked.

"Everything is good here, as well. Yet, I don't know Paa...I don't know about this feeling that I have been feeling since morning that something is fishy. Something isn't going good somewhere."

"Maybe, you are overthinking, my sweetheart," Mr Singh said, trying to disburden tensity.

"Yes, Paa, hopefully. I feel like crying out loud without any reason. I don't know what's wrong with me. Keeping my fingers crossed that everything should be okay."

"Yes. God bless you, now it's late here. I am going to sleep, will talk to you tomorrow. Bye, sweetheart. Good night."

In the hospital, Dr Krishna came and asked about the patient's recovery.

Doctors said, "No improvement. His condition is still the same. We all are just trying our best."

21st April 1979, in the evening around 7:00 pm, Vineesh woke up and asked the nurse to call his father in the room.

"Your son is conscious now. And he has been calling your name, you can proceed to meet him," One Nurse said to Mr Lal.

Mr Lal entered the room.

"Papa, I am sorry, I am sorry, please forgive me. You and Maa were both right. Please save my life. I want to live now. I understand life's value. I don't want to die. I should have talked to you or anyone about my depression. Please help me. I want to go home. I want to sleep on my mother's lap once again. Papa, I am not able to breathe properly," He held Mr Lal's hand and called his name "PAA". He seemed like he wanted to talk a lot. "PAA," He couldn't say more to him. He closed his eyes, and he left the world at 09:00 pm. Mr Lal's hand remained on his son's chest. And the echo of his emotions burst out all over the hospital.

Doctors rushed towards Vineesh.

"Dr Krishna, please look at my son. Please save my son. He talked to me. He said he wanted to live. He promised me he would do whatever I would say to him. Please, doctor. Please, save my son."

"Mr Lal, I do understand your emotions, but doctors aren't God. If I were, I would have saved my father. We can only try our best."

All senior doctors were monitoring his heartbeat, but all it showed_____

_____nothing else. *"We couldn't save your son. Sorry, Mr Lal."*

Chapter 15

An Infelicitous

---

*O*n 21st April 1979. At Krishna's home, Gopika and Shelly were preparing food in the kitchen, and they both were discussing the day when she visited the village with Barkha, how the village's nature and its beauty attracts the children! After seeing the beauty of nature, Barkha wasn't ready to come home, and she was too keen to shift the village.

"My innocent baby."

"Hey! my daughter Shelly, what happened? Why do you seem upset?"

"Nothing, Maa."

"What are you trying to hide? I have known you since your Teenage. Stop playing hide and seek. I am your Maa, tell me what's wrong?"

"I am just worried about Krishna. His health, Maa. His profession is like that he can't look after his health. I prepared breakfast for him in the morning, and............" Shelly said.

"What? Didn't he come last night? Did he come early in the morning and leave again in the morning itself? Is it?"

"Yes, Maa, moreover I prepared breakfast for him. He came early this morning and left for his work in an hour, having just two sips of coffee and without any bread and butter."

"I know, Shelly. My son Krishna is passionate about his work. I have known my son so well. He is dedicated."

"Yeah, he said one of his patients is serious."

"Hey! Shelly, what's the time?"

"It's 05:30 pm, but why are you asking the time, Maa?"

"What about Barkha? Where is she? I noticed her as she wasn't keeping well since last night. She slept early also, without listening to the climax of her favourite fairy tales."

"My goodness! Barkha is still sleeping. She usually wakes up early in the morning. I don't know how I could have overlooked it! How could I be so careless! I should go to her room and check on her."

Shelly rushed straight towards her room, and she saw Barkha was still sleeping. She tried hard to wake her up. She didn't move. Hence she removed the blanket to check her condition. What she saw was extremely shocking to her. An ugly fluid was discharging from her ears. When she touched her face to check her temperature, she had a high fever and was unconscious."

Shelly called Krishna at his hospital. As her calls were unanswered, she called an ambulance and took her daughter to the hospital. Gopika stayed home only as she was aged, she wanted to go with them, but she couldn't travel as she was feeling low.

They reached the hospital. Barkha was still sleeping and unconscious.

"Doctor, please check my daughter....please check," Shelly pleaded.

"She was happy last night because she went to the village a few days back. When she came back, we all had dinner together, we made her favourite south Indian dish, after dinner she left for her room. She wakes up early in the morning, whatever it takes, with her Grandmother. She is still sleeping. It's 9 pm. Doctor, what happened to her?" Shelly started crying.

The doctor came and checked on her, and she was unconscious.

"Where is her father, Dr Krishna?" Doctor asked.

"He is in the hospital only. He has one urgent case, so he is busy," Shelly said.

"Oh, he must be unaware that his daughter got admitted to the same hospital." He called in the hospital for Dr Krishna.

At 9:30 pm, Krishna was sitting on a chair, lost in deep thought. He got a call. He answered, his colleague told him everything about his daughter that she got admitted to the same hospital in the evening."

When Krishna got to know that his daughter was admitted to the hospital, he rushed to his daughter's room. As he had just lost one life in front of his eyes, he knew the pain of losing loved ones. He couldn't lose his precious daughter at any cost. Even though he didn't spend much time together with Barkha, she was his entire world. His lifeline.

He entered his daughter's room, "Barkha, wake up my darling, your father is back, your Daddy is here standing right in front of you, my princess. I promise I will have breakfast and dinner with you. I will look after you, my doll."

Krishna was trying to please and talk to his daughter. "Please get up and talk to your daddy. Please get up, my child. Crap! I had seen my father in the hospital and went through a huge trauma for so long. I can't see my little one like this. I can't bear this pain again," He started sobbing.

At 10:30 pm, Barkha woke up. She saw herself in the hospital. Her parents were sitting right outside the cottage room in the hospital.

"Where am I? I want to go to my Mumma. Please call her."

"Hey! Your mother and father were getting worried about you. Tell me honestly, how are you feeling now? I will surely call them to meet you. They have been waiting outside for you to wake up."

She couldn't hear her voice. The Nurse was repeatedly asking, but Barkha kept staring at the nurse's mouth without hearing a single word. She used hand gestures to convey the message to the nurse that she wasn't able to hear anything. And once she was convinced that the nurse understood her, she turned back to sleep and closed her eyes.

The nurse called Barkha's parents sitting outside. They both came inside and asked about her health to the nurse.

"Nothing is serious about her. She kept staring at me, and she didn't say anything. She wanted to talk, but she wasn't able to speak clearly due to weakness, maybe." Nurse said.

Well, Krishna and Shelly entered her room, standing near her bed; they asked, "How are you, my child?" She gave the same hand gesture, which indicated that she couldn't hear anything.

"What is she trying to say, Krishna? Why is she talking to us like this? She is just using hand gestures as if she can't speak or hear us," Shelly hugged her daughter and started crying on her shoulder.

Krishna had already seen one life lost a few hours back. He wasn't able to bear all the pain. He shouted at Shelly, "C'mon, Shelly. Please don't act like this in front of our daughter. You should understand that she will be fine. She must be tired and nothing else, that's why she can't hear or speak anything. That's it."

"I am sorry, Krishna, I swear, I didn't want to create any scene in front of our daughter. Seeing her condition and being her mother, I am worried about her. She will be fine but not is, please...please save my daughter, just save our daughter, Krishna. I want to see her like before. I want her back to how she felt at the top of the world when she returned from the village. She was absolutely fine the day before yesterday. She was making us laugh so much and making fun of her grandmother at the time of dinner. I can't see her like this," Shelly said.

"Love, control yourself. She isn't deaf. She is tired. She isn't deaf. Our daughter is healthy and fine. And I promise she will live a healthy life. Trust me."

The next day till the afternoon, there was no improvement in Barkha's health. In the evening, at around 6:00 pm, Krishna called one of his doctor friends, working in the same hospital named Dr Saxena (ENT Specialist).

"Doc, I want to save my daughter at any cost and whatever it takes. She is the reason that we smile. We can't see losing her life and living her whole life as a deaf person. She has her whole life ahead. She is so young."

Dr Saxena kept her under observation for one week. He didn't allow her family members to visit and see her. One week later, Krishna asked Dr Saxena, "When can I meet my daughter?"

"Thanks Krishna for calling me. I was about to call you to tell you that I have not been able to find the root of her disease yet. I don't know what's wrong with her. I couldn't find the reason for her hearing loss. Yet, I couldn't find any improvement in Barkha's hearing either. As far as I observed her condition, she completely lost her hearing. She isn't mute. She can speak, but due to her earache, she is trying to avoid speaking. I am sorry to say this made her mute as well." Dr Saxena referred Barkha to his senior, Dr Goel.

They took Barkha to Dr Goel (Sr. ENT Specialist), referred by Dr Saxena. It had been few years, and there was no improvement seen in Barkha. Her education was getting affected by her poor health. After trying several specialists, Gopika and Shelly gave up on her and accepted that she would live her whole life being deaf.

Krishna was a doctor seeing his daughter in the hospital, couldn't bear the pain, in such a condition, "She is my lifeline. I can't handle my daughter's sickness. What is the cause of her disability? Why does no one even know the roots of her ill health?"

Krishna couldn't understand anything. He wanted someone to talk to and suggest something right about his daughter. Hence made a call to Prof Roy. He was Krishna's best friend. Krishna considered him like his elder brother. Prof Roy used to live in the USA. So due to the different time zone, he didn't take the call. Krishna didn't try again and left a message for him.

At 11:00 pm in the night, he got a call from the USA. Prof Roy asked Krishna to bring Barkha to the US for her treatment as no improvements were in her condition. Prof Roy loved Barkha and pampered her more than his children. He had been spoiling Barkha by giving her lots of gifts, dozens of chocolate and flowers especially, all the way from the US. One of her favourite gifts was a 4ft tall Barbie doll, which she got on her 5th Birthday. She liked it so much that she couldn't live without it.

Prof Roy lived in the USA along with his son and wife. Whenever he came to India, he met Krishna and his family without fail, especially to eat crispy Onion Pakoda (Fritters) and Veg Biryani (Rice Dish) with Yoghurt prepared by Shelly. She was a Chef and being a good cook, she loved to keep her kitchen extremely clean and hygienic. Prof Roy and his family used to spend several hours at Krishna's house only. They all became good family friends and couldn't ask for more.

Being a father, Krishna didn't give up. His last hope was to take her to the US for treatment. Hence Krishna called Prof Roy and asked about the whole expenses for the treatment. He was about to travel to the USA along with his daughter next week. After hours of discussion with Prof Roy, Krishna got determined to take his daughter to the USA.

Further, Prof Roy asked him to send Barkha's report via Fax to make an appointment with the next available doctor.

Krishna faxed her reports to Prof Roy and waited for the appointment. All the formalities and lengthy procedures took its time.

Barkha's new best friends are an ancient kaleidoscope ballpoint pen, an elegant eye-pleasing salmon pink colour notebook with a glitter butterfly on its cover. Her conversation was in writing form. She was living like a deaf, although she wasn't mute when she tried to speak something, she feels severe pain in her ear and jaw, therefore, she started interacting herself writing on a notepad. Her conversation mode became a writing pad.

"Barkha, my darling child, get ready to fly to the USA," Her father wrote.

Barkha was on cloud 9. She wrote, "Oh, wow! The USA. My dream place? A well-developed country, I heard everything good about it. If destiny gives me a chance to shift to any country, I will go with the USA after India. I just love it."

And after thinking for five minutes, she wrote again, "I don't want to go anywhere other than this house. I Love you, Daddy. You did a lot for me. You are the world's best father ever. You still haven't lost hope and never give up on me. Yet, now I have given up on everything. I want to stay home only. It's okay that I won't go to school for my further education. I will stay home the whole day. I will do household work with Mumma and will assist my grandmother in the kitchen.

I will keep myself busy to learn some culinary art, and I will be happy doing this. I will start practising mindfulness to keep myself focused and avoid depression. Being your obedient daughter, I would love to be honest, Dad! I am sick of travelling door to door, hospital to hospital, rooms to rooms, here to there, ups and downs. And thousands of strange, scary machines. I want to stay home only. I want some relaxation of my mind and tiring body. Daddy!! I still venerated myself that I have got a father like you. Many kids outside don't even have a family and don't even have a father like you. So what if I lost my hearing for some reason? You, my grandma, and mummy did a lot for me. I will spend the rest of my life with all your support at home only. Still, I feel grateful among all of you, among my family. I am not physically challenged. Yes, maybe a few not well-mannered people living outside would comment, bully me on my hearing impairment, although my pure soul can never be physically challenged.

Moreover, the other day, I read one article that motivated me a lot during this challenging time that physically challenged are not physically defected. Physically challenged are those who have eyes but can't see their blessings and the positive sides of beautiful lives, who have a tongue but don't have the courage to speak the truth, and misuse it to criticize and bully people all the time. Who uses abusive words, who have healthy hands but raise their hands to beat children and women, but not to help people in need. Who has a heart but involves into unnecessary fights and create violence to pretend themselves brave, who don't have kindness in heart to forgive people, who don't respect senior citizens, who have ears but don't have time to listen to morning prayers, who has a healthy body but misuse their entire life procrastinating and complaining every time even after having privileged life, who have feet but run away leaving their old parents. Hence in this manner, I am not physically challenged, Daddy."

"You want to say something more, or that's it?" Dr Krishna continued, "Well, fantastic thinking. I respect your compassionate heart and maturity, but How would you live without hearing my voice and without listening to any voice?" Dr Krishna wrote her back.

She wrote again: "I will be fine. Don't overthink. Now come on, give me a magical daddy hug. And I want to sleep on your lap for some time. Can I ?"

Seeing his daughter's mature heart, Krishna, down in the dumps, cried out loud, pampering his daughter, "I am sorry, my princess. I hate the doctor degree that I cannot be helping you out from this tough situation. I am feeling so helpless. Yes, you were right that my girl is not physically challenged. You are my world's best daughter. You are my perfect little princess. You deserve to be treated like a princess."

"Everyone deserves to be respected, and every girl deserves to be treated like a princess." She wrote.

"Yes, my daughter. You won." He wrote.

Chapter 16

A Miracle

On 07th October 1981

*T*he occasion of the Navratri festival that spans nine nights and is celebrated every year in the autumn when Goddess Durga is worshipped. On day nine, everyone was celebrating the Navratri festival outside of Barkha's house. In the evening, she was sleeping inside her room, and she woke up hearing some noise. She heard some noise coming from outside from the window. She got up, hearing the noise of loudspeakers and the beat of the drum. She went to the window to look out. People were celebrating Durga Puja. She heard the noise of loudspeakers. She could hear it.

"Miracles happen every day," She smiled and whispered to herself.

She went downstairs, "Grandma, ask me anything. I would answer it. I can hear, I can hear everything again, after years of the struggle I got my hearing back. Now, I can hear stories with your soft voice again. We can live in fairy tales once again, our better time has arrived."

Dumbstruck, Gopika looked at her, "Oh my Gosh! Say that again! You just spoke! I mean, you are speaking! Speaking to me! That's a true blessing from almighty God, sweetie, I am glad to know, but I just can't believe it. Your tough time is over. Yes, this is our time. Let me call your name Barkha, can you hear it? Let me pinch myself. Why are you standing so far away? Come closer. I want to hug you hard, and I want to scream out to the world that my Barkha can hear me back, let me hug you, let me call to your Daddy, let me call to your Mamma, let me tell the entire universe that my Grandchild can hear back my fairy tales." Gopika broke down, crying tears of joy. "I am sorry again, but I still can't believe my doll. Patience, good intentions, a genuine prayer from a pure heart paid off. Its credit goes to the almighty lord, then especially your father, who didn't lose hope. Let me call your Daddy, now."

"I am so glad grandma, Even I can't believe this miracle, but all your efforts and prayers have been answered."

"Yes, my sweetheart. We all are happy for you. Let's celebrate," Gopika hugged her tightly.

Shelly came from the kitchen and saw Gopika and Barkha were crying, cuddling each other. So she asked, "Hey, what's going on here? What's the matter? And Barkha, what are you still doing downstairs? Go to sleep?"

"No, mamma, we will binge eat together tonight. I don't want to sleep at this time."

"No way, I will send your dinner to your room only. You are not well. Go to your room right now."

Barkha and Gopika both kept staring- mysteriously at Shelly. They both were smiling to see each other's faces.

"What! Why are you both smiling! Wait a minute, how come! Did you just answer me! Oh my goodness! Let me pinch myself! Just say that again, call me mummy & say that again that you will have dinner together. Oh lord! I am grateful that my daughter is left with no ear disorders. I have been waiting for this day for my little one. I don't have words to say as of now. I am just overwhelmed, I can't express my feelings except loads of blessings for you, and I am grateful for those prayers which have become true. How long we have waited for this day to come. This is a miracle, Maa." She knelt down on the floor and started sobbing like a newborn.

Krishna comes in the evening. It was not obvious to him as he wasn't aware that her daughter's ear disease had resolved entirely on its own.

"Prof Roy called me this afternoon and confirmed the doctor's appointment. Get ready for travelling to the USA, my doll. We are soon heading to your dream country." He still didn't lose hope.

"Now, we don't need to travel to the USA." Shelly and Gopika said.

"Why? She must be denying it only, I know. I can't afford to see her living like this for the rest of her entire life, though." Krishna said.

"Yes, I deny it because I can hear your mellifluous voice once again, Daddy. You are amazing, and you never give up on me. I can never pay for whatever you all did for me." She poured her heart out with ambivalent emotions.

An absolute emotional evening for the entire family. Everyone in the house had tears of joy. The whole family celebrated Durga Puja together. A divine, blissful evening for everyone.

The next day at breakfast, Barkha asked Krishna for a gift.

"Gift? My doll, all yours, just say what do you want?"

"Daddy, I want one month's beach vacation along with you, Grandma, and mamma. I want to go south, Kanyakumari.

I know you all suffered a lot for me. I have a few memories with you. I want to collect more," she said.

"Hey, that's fantastic. We will go soon, surely. Maybe next year."

"Daddy, you want me to be deaf again?"

"Hey, my sweetie, anything for you. Never say that again. We will go next week. And I will spend a month with all of you. Especially my loving daughter Barkha. I promise."

And one month later, they returned to their hometown from Kanyakumari with lots of untroubled memories. They all once again started living like a perfect happy family at their house, so-called a fun kingdom with a beautiful, charming princess.

Barkha got her hearing back, and she spent one month with her family. Now she wanted to learn something to enhance her talent and shape up her career once again. She liked fashion designing; hence she enrolled herself at the nearest designing Institute.

She was learning to stitch and practising for hours at her home and institute as well. However, she was not content as she couldn't complete her academic education due to her early age of illness. She gazed out of her room's window, seeing a group of girls of her age wearing school uniforms, going to school and college.

Although she was no longer left with hearing loss, she felt like a special child without completing her academic education. Even though she was the daughter of a well-reputed doctor in the town, she felt like an underprivileged girl. She lost all hope to achieve something great in her life. She accepted whatever life comes with next, be it a surprising fairytale lifestyle or a death as a gift. I would accept every life's challenges.

Chapter 17

A Promise

On 1st January 1985, Gopika held a New Year party at her home. She invited her relatives and her childhood friends from her village to attend the party. She was waiting for her special guest, her childhood friend Sumita. When she arrived at the venue, Gopika got overwhelmed to meet her.

"Hey, Gopika! you are looking so old and pale, are you fine?" Sumita said.

Sumita and Gopika had grown together, and both still maintain the same bond as best friends since their childhood.

"Yes, I am absolutely fine," Gopika said.

Sumita had come with her grandson Inder, dark-skinned, 5'8"ft. 21yrs, old. Gopika asked Sumita about Inder as she wanted to know what he had been studying. Sumita started narrating his career "Oh! He is so brilliant and secured good rankings in physics, chemistry and mathematics. He will be heading to the USA for his business school. After completing his study, he will be returning to start his business in India only. He wants to be an entrepreneur."

"An Entrepreneur?"

"He wants to be a Businessman."

"Oh! I am sorry, yes, I can see his personality."

Gopika was feeling blue that day; everyone was so busy attending to guests. Hence no one had noticed her health except Inder. Thus he offered her a glass of water to drink. His intellectual and caring personality influenced Gopika. She asked Sumita if she was looking for a girl for him to marry? Sumita shook her head in negative terms. No, not yet. To be honest with you, he is studious, introverted and not into marriage at all. I can't talk to him about it. He will be flying soon, and there is no chance left for him to get settled here with a girl. I know him; he can't see anything interesting other than his career. I wonder! How he got ready to come here with me! Otherwise, he is committed to his dreams only. I don't even think he'd ever get married."

In family gathering and interacting with her old friend Sumita from her village, which she left years ago, hence Gopika got emotional. They both lost themselves in their childhood memories like how they both used to play whole day in the mud at the riverside, how they learnt to prepare food first time; during their conversation in her zeal, Gopika asked for a promise from her childhood friend Sumita, "I would like my granddaughter to marry your grandson Inder as soon as possible."

The evening party was over, and all guests went home. Krishna and Shelly were collecting gifts, flower bouquets brought by their precious guests, especially white roses, as Barkha loved a bunch of white roses. They saw Gopika sitting in the corner on the chair. Barkha moved towards Gopika to listen to fairy tales. Grand ma fainted on the floor as she touched her shoulder randomly.

Krishna got into flashback memories as he lost his Baba like this only, he took her to the nearest hospital. Gopika had contracted a severe injury in her lower spine that she was hiding for so long. She got admitted. Around 1:00 am at midnight, she called Krishna, who was sitting outside her room. She asked him to sit near her bed.

She held his hand, "We have acres of land in our village. We never thought about making any will as it was all yours only. You can take my words as my will. I want to give 20% of the precious gem of land to my Granddaughter Barkha on her day of the wedding, and the remaining Land in charity to build a school for the bright future of children living in the village. To educate them about gender equality as we made one mistake when you were a newborn. The charity is to justify that mistake."

"Maa as you wish. I will do the paperwork soon. However, I don't know why you are talking like this?"

"Do you know my age? I am still alive because of the love you gave me."

"Maa, we need you forever. You are our real wealth. Barkha doesn't need anything from you. I will be happier if you give everything to charity to needy people if you want to. You and Baba made your son adequately independent to look after his family and to fulfil their wishes. I am not rapacious."

"Now, who is talking rubbish? Consider it my blessings to Barkha. Stop arguing with me. Just one more thing I love to share is I gave my childhood friend Sumita a promise that I will get my granddaughter Barkha married to her grandson Inder."

Krishna lost his cool, "Maa, what are you talking about now? Did you discuss this with Barkha and Shelly?"

"Inder is a good and caring person. I saw him last night at the party."

"Maa, Why did you do this? Maa, you know Barkha is a vulnerable soul. I can't send her away from my heart, and our Village is too far," Krishna said.

"This is my last wish," Gopika said.

"I don't know Maa, you know Shelly, she won't be convinced without asking consent of girl and boy, both. Anyway, I will try to convince them."

"That's my boy. Please show me your father's picture. It must be in your wallet, I know."

Krishna placed his father's picture on his mother's palm. She kept staring at Nand's photograph, "I am coming to you," she took her last breath to leave the world peacefully. She left forever.

Krishna silently kept staring at his mother, holding her palm. Krishna lost in flashback memories of how he teased his Baba and Maa, how soon a little Krishna had grown up and his parents left him. Crucial truth of life, how time flies by. He felt like an orphan. He lost two gems out of his life's treasure. He had no courage left to call his home to let his wife know about it, and he didn't know how Barkha would react to it. She is still naïve to understand the reality of death and to bear its pain. Somehow, he managed to take his colleague's help to call home to let Shelly know about Gopika's sad demise.

Shelly lost her world, her Kitchen - Companion. "I don't know how we would let Barkha know about this? I accepted this crucial truth of death to convince myself as Maa was too old and getting sick day by day. Barkha will collapse knowing about her grandma. Moreover, She had just recovered from her past disease, and she went through lots of mental challenges. This would be a huge trauma to her life. She is close to her Grandma; her chatterbox left the world, left Barkha alone, and left all of us alone."

"Whom are you talking to overcall? Why would I collapse? What are you hiding Mummy? Where is Daddy? I haven't seen him since this morning. Daddy must be in the hospital at this time. What about Grandma, Oh! Yeah, she had fainted last night. Is she fine now? Where is she? She never goes anywhere without taking me. Tell me, Maa. I want to listen to fairytales from her. Why are you crying, Mummy? I want to know the climax, a story's climax, a climax she had left a day before. Where is my Grandma?" Barkha couldn't remain silent without asking about her Grandma.

Meanwhile, Krishna entered his home with her Mother's dead body wrapped and covered with a white cotton cloth. Krishna didn't uncover it from her face, just to not let Barkha know about it. Her parents could only manage to tell Barkha that "Grandma is sleeping now and asked us not to disturb her. Grandma has vanished now, and she has become a star in the galaxy."

Barkha saw her Grandma. She has never seen a dead body yet, so she couldn't understand why she is sleeping like this. She couldn't even cry. She was in huge shock about why she vanished without letting me know. She couldn't get over it for so long. Her parent's later decided to get their daughter married as per their Maa's last wish. Eventually, they convinced everyone, and they got their daughter married in a small gathering. It was a simple wedding ceremony among closest relatives and friends.

Chapter 18

A Shooting Star

On 12th December 1986, after Barkha's marriage, she moved to the village at Inder's House. Barkha accepted the environment of the village. Yet she used to miss her house in the Town often. Barkha had a childlike innocence and was a bubbly girl. She loved to spend her whole day sitting by the riverside. She loved hanging out at the small farm she had inherited. She loved to be in nature. She loved to listen to the sound of bird's chirping, sometimes a soft compose chirp and sometimes a soft musical whistle. She loved to count birds sitting at trees one by one. And at night, she loved to count stars. She became a good swimmer, and she loved swimming. She used to dive deeper into the river to explore the inside world of water. She wanted to fly like a bird, go to the moon, and build her hut shaped house over there. She had a dream, yet she couldn't tell anyone about her dream, not even to her parents, not to her husband, Inder. Sometimes she used to talk to herself, "I don't feel like talking about my dream to anyone. My dream no longer exists anymore. The galaxy of my dream is diluted in the colour of the dark sky. Whenever

I look at the sky, I see if there is any meteor shower so that I can ask a wish for my dream, a dream – 'Ashiana'.

A white coloured, wood hut shaped exterior, grey, blush pink, rose gold interior, oval-shaped glass windows and doors decorated with beautiful white curtains—an outdoor infinity pool with kitchen surrounded by several types of trees and white - pink rose garden. No neighbourhood. I want all possible amenities in my small elegant kingdom, where I can avail and explore everything that I don't feel like to go anywhere outside of my world – 'Ashiana'. My dream house remained in my sweet dreams only. How painful is it, to accept that I can't even fulfil my only one dream – Ashiana." Meanwhile, talking to herself, she gazed at the sky, she saw one meteor star, but she overlooked it.

She often missed one day of her life a lot, that she came to the village first time with her grandmother and asked her to shift in the village. "How everything was so quintessential at that time when my dream seemed so perfect as it would come true one day. The reality of life suck," She whispered while heading towards her home.

She didn't like doing chores and household activities as she had never done this before at her own house. She hated it.

Even though she was newly married, her relationship with Inder wasn't perfect like a fairy tale. It was utterly monotonous.

Everything she dreamt of her marriage was going in the opposite direction. The fun fact is this couple didn't even fight.

"What sort of relationship is this? Just dull and worst. Not healthy like my parents' life. Just worst..worst. My married life is becoming hell, Grandma. No prince is charming in reality. Everything seems soulless."

She couldn't accept this marriage & couldn't understand why grandma gave that promise to her childhood friend without asking her, moreover she was too close to her. It was least acceptable for Barkha as Gopika was attentive towards her upbringing, good education. She got furious when Barkha demanded she shifts to the village along with her. While thinking about all flashback memories, she gazed at the sky and yelled, "Why did you do this? Why? Grandma, this was a big decision of someone's life without asking anyone, especially me. To my parents as well as. Inder and my relationship is not healthy. We are not even compatible with each other. He only behaved nicely on the day of marriage, that's it, and the rest is history."

A year and a few months later, Barkha's Family: Shelly, Krishna and Prof Roy arrived in the village to meet Barkha on her Birthday to surprise her. They got good news from her mother in law. Barkha was three and a half months pregnant. They said to each other, "We came to surprise her, but Barkha surprised us. How my little princess is a responsible woman today, and soon she will become a mother."

However, Barkha was looking pale. Prof Roy asked, "Why are you upset? You should be happy that you are soon going to be a mother and thankful to your Grandmother that she saved your life and fulfilled your wish."

Barkha looked at him surprisingly, "How come Grandma saved my life and fulfilled my wish?"

Prof Roy said, "When you were young and lost your hearing, I consulted one of the best specialists about your health and shared your report after scrutinizing your issues. He suggested that your immune system is weak as well, and you should be surrounded by fresh air and eating organic food, i.e. green vegetables and fruits, all diseases can be cured."

"I communicated the same to your grandmother Gopika and had a long conversation over the phone that day. She knew that you wanted to shift in the village, and you would hang out on the farm where you went to in your childhood with your grandmother once. So this is why she decided to get you married in the village only."

Barkha gazed at the sky and said, "Oh! So, this was the reason that you made me marry Inder. Thank you, Grandma, for being the world's best. And you proved it, yet again."

Barkha shared something with Prof Roy, "I feel blessed to have everything and good people around me. However, I am not comfortable with Inder and his family. I am not complaining about them and their behaviour towards me. However, there are compatibility issues. My choices and theirs are so different. My way of living life and theirs are not equal. The way I see the world, a perfect world, but they don't make it perfect. I spend my whole day at the riverside and lose myself in beautiful memories. Inder usually leaves for his work early in the morning and comes late. His parents remain busy with their friends and relatives, cooking food, hanging out with neighbours, attending fairs, shopping. For me, there is no one to talk to throughout the whole day. I feel lonely most of the time. I used to be a free spirit, a little outgoing, extrovert at my home with Mumma, Papa and Grandma. For many days I wanted to talk to someone about this matter, but I had no courage. I haven't shared this with my parents yet, and they would get tensed to know that their daughter is not comfortable with her in-laws, especially with her husband, Inder. I have not been able to accept this sudden change in my life. First marriage to an unknown guy, we both are not compatible with each other, and now I am expecting a child."

Prof Roy tried to convince her, "Every girl has to face this sudden change. This is quite normal. After the baby delivery, you can come to the USA to enhance your skills in designing and to a great start-up. In the USA your life will become more happening then, and you too will be busy with your work. I will discuss this with your father, Krishna."

Barkha said, "No, don't. Never share this with my parents. You can't tell them that their daughter is not happy at her in-law's house. I don't want my parents to know about all this. I only want someone to listen to me and be all ears. That's why I poured my heart out to you. And thanks, Roy uncle, for hearing me out. Being a married woman and soon to be mother, it's not right for me to shift to the US. I believe it needs a lot of money to travel and shift there. Initially, I don't want financial help from my parents or in-laws to go to the USA as Inder doesn't like taking help from parents. He has a big ego and self-respect.

Moreover, Inder is planning the same. He won't allow me to go alone. I will enhance my clothes designing skills living here only and start my own small business. I don't want to hurt Inder's self-respect."

Prof Roy observed that Barkha had lost weight, and she was not happy at Inder's house. He didn't know how to help her. He got upset, too, as Barkha was still like his doll. However, he agreed to Barkha's traditional thoughts that despite not being content, she wants to live with her in-laws only and can't go against and beyond her spouse's self-respect.

"This is rare. What a maturity in her," Prof Roy whispered. Somewhere Prof Roy knows the reason behind her decision why she doesn't want to leave her spouse's house. This girl is still living in fairytales and believes in them. Her Grandma once told her in her stories that a True Queen never returns to her parental home after marriage and never leaves her king till death at any cost. It's her duty and right. In this modern era, Barkha's moral and better upbringing melted Prof Roy's heart, and he touched her feet in respect without letting her know. He gave her a lot of blessings and to her unborn child.

They took their leave from the house along with Barkha's parents. Prof Roy was driving his car, Krishna was sitting next to him, and Shelly sat in the back seat. They started cracking jokes and gossiping about Barkha, saying that their daughter looked pretty and was a lady now. Prof Roy wasn't indulged in their conversation as he was a bit upset to know about his daughter's non-happening marriage life. As he promised that he wouldn't share anything with her parents, he remained silent and kept driving.

Barkha and her mother-in-law went to the temple for routine prayers every morning. Barkha's mother in law belongs to the traditional family, so she followed old rituals and culture. Barkha was feeling anxious and preoccupied. In the evening, Barkha got a call that her parents had an accident last night and were hospitalized. The doctor refused her to travel. She couldn't understand how to look after and meet her parents. She called Inder working in the town and asked him to meet her parents as they had an accident last night while departing from here. When he came home, Barkha asked Inder about her parent's health. Inder said, "I was busy with my international delegates as I have to go to the USA asap. It was related to an urgent meeting about business expansion with an aviation group. The whole day was so tiring and then I came straight home. I didn't feel like stopping in between and almost forgot to meet. Sorry, love. We will both go tomorrow in the morning, surely. It was a hectic day. I need to go to sleep, Goodnight."

Barkha couldn't control her emotions and burst out loud on Inder for the first time. "How come a person can be so casual in his personal life, even when his wife's parents are hospitalized!? How could you come home without meeting my parents!? You evildoer, self-seeking, stone-hearted person!? How come a person can leave their parents when they need their kids the most!? Will both go tomorrow!? Are you serious!? Oh lord! This guy didn't even know that his expecting wife was not allowed to travel anywhere. They had an accident, and I couldn't even eat anything due to anxiety. I kept praying for them. I have been thinking and waiting for you, the whole day, you would come with some news about the parents. I don't even know what they both are suffering from, how much did they hurt! The doctor refused me to travel so I couldn't go to see them. This is why I informed you in time and almost didn't expect you to come up with an excuse. Now you are escaping by giving just simple excuses saying that you forgot and had no time. What the hell, Inder! They are not random people. They gave me this life. Whatever I am today, it's only because of my parents. They are my parents, not strangers. Do you even know what you have done? I never complained anything about the lack of compatibility in our so-called married life. I have never been happy at your house since the day after our marriage. I have been living here with you and your parents because I respect my grandmother's choice. She is no more, so I couldn't go beyond her wish. Being their son-in-law, they too have some expectations from you same as your parents have from me. My parents never asked me for anything, but they need me at this time, and I can't go to meet them.

"I am afraid, will go by tomorrow morning, surely," Inder replied casually.

Barkha was displeased with Inder's behaviour. "I don't want to listen to any single word. Not even false empathy. I know you are still not feeling guilty. I want to know this. Why morning!? Why would you visit them in the morning!? They have been in the hospital since last night. They have no one to look after them and will go to meet them tomorrow? I am still not sure that you would go. I am leaving you Inder and your house, right at this moment. I can handle my traumas, but I can't tolerate the fact that parents are alone in the hospital and you didn't visit them, as they don't have their loved ones with them in their hard times visit them. They need us this time. This is non-negotiable. I always wanted to be a Queen, but I forgot that I needed a King first to be a Queen.

Chapter 19

An Emptiness

On 16th July 1987, At midnight, Barkha left Inder's house without telling anyone. She spent her whole night sitting outside the temple. She was crying, missing her Grandma, her parents, and she kept sobbing the entire night, as she was expecting and due to overstress, she fainted outside the temple.

Few people who knew her took her to the hospital. Eventually, it was the same hospital where her parents got admitted. She got her consciousness back and requested nurses to take her to her parent's room to meet them.

She got a minor fracture in her ankle last night. Hence nurse took her in a wheelchair to meet her parents. The nurse said, "Dr Krishna and Prof Roy got a severe internal injury in the head. Your mother also got conscious this morning only. But by god's grace, she is out of danger now.

They both lost too much blood and fluid from their body and are still unconscious. We have to operate them. We have all been waiting for you or any closest family members for a long time to come here and visit them. As you know, the hospital has its own rules & regulations that we are bound to conclude its formalities, without it we can't go ahead for anything. Hospitals need authority first. We already wasted time," The nurse mentioned this rudely.

"Do you know my father? My father, Dr Krishna, is already a top surgeon by himself. He doesn't even need any authority to operate on him." Her voice was shaky due to several anxieties.

Meanwhile, the nurse handed over a form to Barkha, and she was told to fill and sign it. A formality that gives an authority to operate. The doctor took Prof Roy and Krishna to the operation theatre. Barkha was sitting near Shelly's bed. Shelly had bruises on her head and elbow. Barkha saw her parents cheerful a day before yesterday, no one could even imagine this misery going to happen, and this mishap was coming their way next. Isn't it scary? What an unpredictable life!

A few hours later, doctors and nurses came outside of the operation theatre. They were standing speechless. Before Barkha and Shelly could ask anything or observe the reason behind their silence, meanwhile, they saw some people behind doctors are coming towards them scrolling two stretchers, full body head to toe covered with white cotton clothes. The same scene she saw the first time when she lost her Grandma. Shelly & Barkha both lost their entire world. After her Grandma, two strong pillars of Barkha's life were no more. It was a dark day for both of them. Barkha blamed herself that she could have saved both lives if she would have come on time.

She couldn't control her emotions and screamed out loud, calling her father's name. Shelly was trying to console and wiped her tears. Both couldn't accept the fact that Shelly lost her love of life, and Barkha lost her entire world. She felt emptiness everywhere. Barkha didn't want to say anything about what she was facing with Inder. She tried to hide about

Inder from her mother. She was not in her senses. She could only manage to say, "I want to shift in the town to look after you." She never wanted to go to Inder's house again in the future. And never wanted to meet Inder ever again. The day she left Inder's house, she left it forever.

She started living in the town with her mother and never returned to Inder. Shelly was upset over Barkha's big decision. She left her husband in a minor conflict. Barkha was expecting, so she supported her daughter.

Barkha had self-respect. She didn't want to entirely depend on her mother, at least at this stage, whereas her mother needed emotional support.

After Krishna's death, Shelly had not been able to get over the demise of her love. She had been with him since a teenager. Krishna's love and struggle to be with Shelly. Such love was rare. It was a true love story. Shelly thought of heading to the USA to live at her brother's house as her entire family had shifted there. Mr Singh and Mrs Sayukta Devi were also living there. Except for Buzo. After Shelly's marriage, Mr Singh gave Buzo to the neighbour as no one was left to play with Buzo. Buzo loved playing with children.

In the evening, around 8 pm, she got a call from the USA. This was a call from her brother Rubal.

"Hey, Rubi!! I have been thinking about you only. What perfect timing!"

"I knew you must be missing me."

"Yeah, well, what's up, my Brother! You are like a pure Rubi," she pretended like everything was fine with her, but it wasn't.

"Why do you sound upset! You must be missing Krishna, right?"

"Mmmm…maybe yes, but I secured him in my heart like a shining star forever."

"Woah! Please come to live with us. Do you know, I left my previous job? And now I have a new big office here—a new big house, my new big car, what I dreamed of. I want to show you around. I want to show you everything I achieved here with the blessing of our beloved Maa-Paa. Please come. I know you can't live without Krishna. I know that you need a change. Please do us a favour and come to the USA. I must say that we are lucky kids that our parents prioritise their health first before anything, that's why they are still fit and fine at their old age. But I like to be honest with you. They are dependent on me now. They need both of us to look after them. It's a request to you to come and look after them. I would say we are one of those blessed people that we got a chance to look after our parents," He said.

He continued……. "You would love the whole atmosphere here. This place!…this place is just… so wow, I am telling you. I will arrange your travel to come over. We would live together over here like we used to live before your marriage with our Maa, Paa. And it would be an honour to look after them. Please come," He insisted, "Just say yes…… say yes that you would come here to live with us. I will arrange your travel, don't worry about anything."

"No…Rubi, I know it's hard to live here without Krishna. Yet, I have responsibilities. Barkha is expecting and all alone here. I can't come. I will come next year. I promise," She wanted to go but refused.

Her daughter Barkha heard that she was talking to someone over the phone. She asked, "Maa, who are you talking to?"

"It's my brother from the USA. He is asking me to shift there. Just forget about it. I am not going anywhere."

"No, Maa. You should go. You can go. Don't worry about me. I am absolutely fine. I will cope with the situation here. I have all the essential contacts. I would call them if needed." That moment Barkha felt a baby kick inside her womb. She didn't react.

"Are you sure, my girl?"

"Damn sure."

"May God bless you, my child. I know it would be cruel, so I will never forgive myself for leaving you at this time, but it's harder to live here without your Daddy. The fragrance of him in this house kills me every day."

She started getting her packing done to travel to the USA. She packed her clothes, footwear and necessary things along with Krishna and Barkha's photo frame. She got her documentation formalities done with the help of her brother as he sponsored her entire trip and was all set to fly to the USA.

Chapter 20

A Bangle

On 08th October 1987, After two weeks with conversation to her brother, she headed to the USA. Her flight was via Delhi. She didn't know how to board. Hence she asked for help from a lady.

"Hey! Could you please help me to board?"

"Sure, but it's easy; airport staff are kind and helpful, you may go straight to the counter and show them your ticket and visa. They will help you further."

"Oh! Thanks."

"My Pleasure, well! where are you going?"

"I am going to the USA to live with my parents and brother."

"Hey! I am also heading to the USA."

"That's fantastic. You were born in the USA?"

"No, I got the job in the USA."

"WOW! I got company."

"Hey! we have the same type of bangle."

"Yeah, from where you got it!"

"It belongs to my mom-in-law. She gave it to me on the day of my marriage. And where did you get it from?"

"A kind lady visited my home town Kerala, years ago. She blessed me with this."

"What a coincidence. May I know your name?"

"Bella."

After 24 hrs, changing a layover, she finally arrived where her elder brother and Maa-Paa were living in the USA. She never looked back and continued living there only. She never returned to India to Krishna's home ever again. After reaching the USA, she made a call to Barkha.

"Hello, ...Barkha."

"Hello Maa, I hope your journey was comfortable."

"Yeah, it was."

"Maa, I miss everyone. I am unable to sleep. Can you tell me one story, like Grandma?"

"Sure, A French girl abandoned by her step-mother. She left home but had to find a safe place as she was so beautiful. Whoever looked at her face eventually fell in love with her, and a gentleman gifted her a magical red beret with a word written "Bonjour" on it. She met a ghost, and he gave her an oak leaf.......then, hey! Are you listening or not?................... hello.... hello! Oh, She slept, but the baby in her tummy must have listened to my story." She disconnected the call.

Months have passed, Barkha realized that women should be independent and always learn some skills. Women shouldn't be entirely dependent on anyone.

Barkha didn't complete her studies due to her disease, hearing loss at a young age. She lived the life of a deaf person for almost a few years and a few more years spent in recovery of trauma, then minor depression of lost her Grandma. In her teens, she attended a diploma class to learn sewing machines to design clothes; therefore, she had known and had enough knowledge of fashion and designing clothes. Hence she opened a small designer boutique in the garage and used to teach how to stitch clothes to women living in her neighbourhood.

One day she gazed outside the window as a group of girls was going to the school in the uniform as she used to see at her young age. She liked seeing school girls in uniform. She felt regret for not completing her studies.

However, she had beautiful features and a brilliant persona. By seeing her, no one would believe that Barkha was uneducated. Uneducated here means she didn't complete her schooling either. She didn't have any academic degree.

She promised herself, and to her unborn child that she would give a comfortable life to her child.

Barkha completed her nine months. She was dealing with slight labour pain in her lower abdomen since morning. She failed to notice it and didn't take her pain seriously. At the end of the day, she felt her pain increase as if she would die right at that moment. She was in severe pain as she wanted to reach the hospital asap, she tried to call the ambulance. She descended the half staircase to get the landline and fell on the stairs.

At midnight around 03:30 am, she woke up and felt herself in the hospital. Her vision was blurry, and she couldn't speak due to several weaknesses. Still, her blurred vision can see a woman who was her neighbour sitting next to her. She was staring at her as if she was only waiting for her to wake up. Barkha was not in her whole consciousness. She only remembered that she dealt with pain a while ago as if someone fractured her 20 bones at once.

Chapter 21

Innocent Souls

*O*n 31st December 1987, midnight around 02:15:20 am (Thursday), she gave birth to twins, two baby girls, fair complexion, tiny eyes, small - small palms, beautiful hands & feet. Her elder child was born with silky black hair, the same as Barkha with perfect princess-like features. And her five minutes younger one had blonde hair. She was born with an angelic characteristic. And once again, Barkha believed in the miracle. Despite facing all obstacles, she gave birth to two beauties—a real beauty on earth. And now little Barkha had become a mother, and princess Shelly was promoted to Granny.

The next day, she called her mother and gave this good news.

"Congratulations, Maa, you become a Granny of my two baby girls. I have given birth to twins, Maa."

"Hey! Congratulations to you, my strong woman. I am on cloud 9! But I still can't believe the news, my little Barkha has become a Mother, and I am Granny! I wish I were there with them and you. I am sorry that in your tough time I wasn't there. But I will send them loads of gifts as my blessings from the USA."

They both had mixed emotions: joy and sorrow. It was an emotional moment for both in the house. By god's grace, Shelly had better skin genes; therefore, all generations inherited pinkish and glowing skin.

Barkha observed her both children; her elder daughter was born with a healthy weight, whereas the younger one, who had blonde hair, was underweight and had a minor complication in her both eyes. She couldn't open her eyes properly. So Barkha had to visit regularly for checkups with the doctor to improve her daughter's eyes and weight. One day Barkha woke up to her elder daughter's face. That day turned into a lucky one as Barkha found an official approval to start a Fashion Boutique in the garage, and her younger daughter finally opened her eyes, as well. She had ocean blue eyes like any fairy from her Grandma's fairy tales.

Barkha was creative in fashion designing. Since she had no official degree, it was hard to open a professional boutique. She wanted her Boutique to be good. However, she didn't try to find any other place as she didn't want to go outside her house.

She was convinced and ended up with a little boutique in the garage. That day she got official approval to open a good Boutique for designer clothes in the garage. She named her elder daughter Lucky. She celebrated the day like a festival. Barkha made it a routine to see Lucky's face first in the morning without fail. Whenever she wakes up, Lucky should be there with her. Lucky became her reason to be proud & Khwahish became a reason to be joyful.

She visited the Doctor for a final checkup of her younger daughter. And now her younger one too could open her both eyes, and she noticed an improvement in her

109

weight. While coming home from the hospital, she noticed her younger one was curious to know everything about the outer world. She gave her mother a thrilling gesture seeing materialistic things. She was getting exhilarated and elevated. As if she was the only child in the world. She was a newborn, but the way she had been reacting wasn't less than a miracle.

She came home and named her younger one Khwahish as she knew it. A kid's capabilities and talents can be seen when they are newborns. And that day Barkha got to know that she would become a dreamer. Somewhere she was getting worried about her both beautiful daughters. How would she keep both of them protected from evil eyes?

Her elder one first time called her mamma, mamma. One of the best feelings in the world. What an amazing day it was.

"Lemme share this news with my mamma." She called Shelly.

"Maa, Lucky called me mamma for the first time. Maa, what a beautiful feeling it is. I have been celebrating my motherhood. I feel like my life is perfectly complete now. I don't need anything other than my daughters."

"I know, my girl, this is the best feeling ever for a woman. What about Khwahish? Hasn't she called your name yet? She is only five minutes younger than Lucky."

"Yes, Maa, Khwahish is only five minutes younger than Lucky. She hasn't called my name yet..it's a matter of being worried. Let me try to teach her."

"Baby, call me mamma, mamma," She tried to teach Khwahish calling her mamma, mamma. She couldn't pronounce correctly.

The next day in the afternoon, Barkha was sleeping, her younger one called her 'Momsy,' After hearing her voice, she got up.

"What did I hear? Call me again," She looked at her mother, grin softly and tried to speak, "Momsy."

"Baby, it's mamma...call me mamma...not Momsy," Barkha kept trying to correct her daughter, and Khwahish kept calling her mother name Momsy. "Okay! Call me Mom... Call me Mom," She was trying to teach her to address her with the correct name. At least she can speak mom.

"Momsy", She said.

"Okay, call me Momsy. You happy?"

After a few years, her younger one could speak everything easily. But she still couldn't say, Mamma. Strange, not even mom. when she tries to tell the word mom, her tongue automatically slips with the sound "sy." She called her mother Barkha by the name of Momsy. Momsy was a unique word. Barkha loved to be called Momsy by her younger one's sweet innocent voice. She got into the habit of listening to Momsy by Khwahish, and later she stopped correcting her daughter. Therefore, Barkha became Momsy for Khwahish. And mamma for Lucky.

During all these years, she never missed Inder and his family. Even Inder never tried to contact her. She got busy looking after her daughters, playing with them and taking them to her Boutique. She used to take her daughters to the Boutique to look after them as she didn't want to skip the joy of motherhood while working. Her daughters became her entire world. And the only reason to live her life. One lady worker, Sashi, commented on her daughters' beauty during her class, said "Try to keep them in the house only. They both are gorgeous, and I have never seen such charming kids ever in my life to date. Try to keep hiding their beauties.....you know the world."

Barkha got mad at that lady, "They will be safe and protected forever. You don't have to be worried about them. Thanks for your advice."

Barkha arrived home. In the night, while sleeping. Barkha was thinking about that incident. Even though she got mad at her in the class, thinking about her advice, she took it seriously now.

Barkha perceived, and she believed that she was right, her both talented, charming daughters could easily come into sight of evil eyes. The biggest challenge was being a single mother and all alone here. "How would I keep them protected among a half corrupted society? Notwithstanding all obstacles, I want to give them better raising."

All she wanted to do was protect her daughters' lives at any cost. Hence she chose to give them a simple life with her loads of restrictions. She removed all the mirrors from the house so that they didn't even get to know how beautiful they were, especially her younger one, Khwahish. She decided to send them to a school adjoined by her house, and it was a Girl's school. Lucky was earnest & acquiescent. She was the first bencher, always obtained good marks with the first rank in the class. At the same time, Khwahish was mulish & ebullient. She was average in studies but good in sports. She loved to indulge herself in sports activities more than studies. She is fond of bicycles; hence she used to ride a bike at her home only as her mother didn't allow her to go outside anywhere after school.

Despite living in the modern century, Barkha lived with her daughters at her parents' home without any worldly things. Barkha was protective and kept her daughters away from the outer fancy world. She never took her daughters to the cinema hall, never to eat in fancy restaurants, they never made any friends in the school. And no birthday parties for them. Their lives revolved around Home - School - and spending quality time with Mamma and sometimes Granny over call. That's it.

They were being bullied, especially Khwahish, in the school. She had blonde hair, ocean blue eyes, so everyone in the school used to tease her. Sometimes for her different hair and eyes colour and sometimes absence of her father at parent-teacher meetings. Some said their father was no more; he died. Some said her father left her mamma and ran away with someone else. Lucky and Khwahish, both at home, spent several hours asking mamma about their father.

"Why doesn't he live with us? What should we answer at school?"

"You both keep your focus on studies and homework. Ignore what your classmate says and asks. That's none of their concern. If required, I will personally come to your school to talk to your principal about all these girls. Don't worry about them, and a request from both of you that we would never discuss this matter ever again in the future as well."

Barkha raised her both daughters like rich kids. Rich means not spoiling them with lots of wealth, unwanted excess toys, fancy clothes and gifts. Yet, she raised her daughters by feeding them all good manners and discipline. She taught them the importance of moral values, such as integrity, determination, loyalty, truthfulness, honesty, and respect for every human being and what is good and bad for them as well as society.

Barkha was struggling hard to raise her daughters Lucky and Khwahish. She was only worried about their future & professional life, along with their safety concern, which was on her top priority list.

She raised her daughters perfectly as she promised them before their birth. One day she was checking her daughter's homework. She noticed one notebook lying on the floor separately. She picked it up and opened it. The first pages were blank, but the last 3-4 pages had handmade drawings of family picnics with her father, parents-teacher meetings with her father, birthday celebration with her father, her father is in the car to drop and pick from the school by father. At the end of one black page, she had mentioned, "Love you, FATHER." She chose a black page to write it to hide her emotions. How much she misses her father in her life.

Khwahish's innocent heart didn't even know that usually, children call their father "papa" or "daddy." Her innocent mind assumed that her father should be addressed by the name "Father" only. However, a strong Barkha didn't take those drawings grievously. She ignored them, as usual.

After Krishna and Prof Roy's death, she wasn't ready to forgive Inder or to even think about him. Whatever it takes, Inder's chapter in her life story completely vanished for her. Inder didn't exist for her. She didn't want to recall anything about it.

Chapter 22

An Apple Lover

*Y*ears have passed. On 31st December 2002, her both daughters completed their 15 years successfully, by the grace of God and efforts.

Barkha threw a small birthday party for Lucky and Khwahish. Shelly insisted on making their 15th birthday special. Barkha invited only those women who were working under her at her Boutique.

They both wore handmade pink designer, floor-length satin evening gowns that Barkha had stitched for the daughters' birthday. It took six months to get the stitching done. Lucky grew up and had shoulder-length black hair, a fair complexion, 5'7" ft tall, wide smile, beautiful features with a decent persona.

Khwahish had knee-length blonde hair. She tied her hair with a bow tie headband. Pretty features, mischievous crooked smile, tiny ocean blue eyes, pink lips, 5'6" ft tall. She was looking like a cinderella.

The best thing about both girls was they didn't need to put on any makeup.

Barkha asked the photographer to take their pictures together. Barkha was fond of apples. She loved apples in fruits a lot. If she could, she would have acquired an entire apple farm. Barkha had an excellent photography sense. So she asked her both daughters to hold a basket filled with apples in their hands then clicked photographs. Barkha was fond of photography. She protected her photo album like it was her assets of gold and diamond. She kept her photograph album in her mother Shelly's closet and told them that it belonged to her mother. She wanted to hide it from her daughters. She never allowed Khwahish and Lucky to go into Shelly's room as she knew Khwahish was adamant. She was only concerned about her rain of questions after seeing those photographs. "Who would bear the pain to answer them? Who had so much time to lose in flashback memories? After all, it was all my past. I should be in the present moment." She murmured.

After Krishna's death, this was the first party held in her house. Hence mother and daughters captured lots of pictures together on their birthday celebration while cutting the cake, eating a piece of cake, sharing laughter and hugging each other. It was one of the best birthdays for Khwahish.

Barkha was protective of her daughters, and she never left them all alone. She noticed that Lucky was busy talking to her guest, but Khwahish was missing. She searched for her in the upstairs hallway, at the terrace, at the balcony, in her room, basement, outside in the garden. She wasn't anywhere.

She sat at the corner of the stairs, "This girl Khwahish is irresponsible..Trust me," she said to Lucky.

"Lemme check outside," Lucky said.

And Lucky moves towards the garden to see her sister. She saw Khwahish standing at the main entrance talking to one man and taking some gifts from that man. His age was around 38-39 yrs old. He came in a huge black car, wearing a formal white suit. She moved towards them to see his face. He was a stranger to her. She called her mother.

"Mamma. We found Khwahish, there she is...she is," She points outside at the main entrance, "She is talking to someone and taking gifts."

Barkha took a sigh of relief, and she came outside. "With whom Khwahish is talking to!" She whispered as Khwahish was visible but the man not. She went closer, and she was flabbergasted. She felt the ground slipping under her feet.

"Inder? What he is doing here," Barkha murmured.

Lucky couldn't understand what was going on, "Inder, who! Who is Inder? Mamma!."

Rather than replying to her question, she shouted at Lucky, "Go inside the house." She pushed her away and moved towards the gate like a lioness as any hunter had attacked her cubs. She came closer to her younger one, as she was in trouble.

"Don't you dare take anything from this man, give everything back to him, whatever he gave to you, give all his gifts back to him right now. We don't take anything from strangers. Come inside."

She looked at Inder aggressively. She was frightened, shocked, and flashback anxiety waved in her face, she could only manage to say in her tremor voice. "You!...what are you doing here! Just……..stay away ……from…… my both daughters ….GO away." She pushed him away. And forcefully closed the main gate & came inside with Lucky and Khwahish.

Khwahish started crying. She couldn't understand what was wrong with her mother. She asked Momsy, "Why did you behave with him like this? He was our guest. And he was talking to me nicely."

"The dumbest girl. Just keep calm and shut your mouth. And don't dare to ask me about that man ever," she replied in aggression.

Lucky and Khwahish looked at each other, they shrugged like, what's wrong with mamma?

Meanwhile, Barkha got a call from the USA. This was her Mother.

"Hello Maa, How are you?"

"I called to wish Birthday to Lucky & Khwahish. May happiness fill their life day by day with joy & prosperity."

"Oh!.. Thanks, Maa. I will convey the message to Lucky."

"To Lucky!"

"Maa, You know Khwahish, so well."

"The reason behind her ignorance?"

"I don't even know the exact reason, but one day I eavesdropped, she was talking to herself that, 'Granny left Momsy when she needed her the most."

"Yeah, I know, but how did she get to know? I left the house at the time when you were expecting."

"I remember a baby kick when you planned to head the USA."

"But she used to give me 7 kisses."

"Yes, I remember, she was 1.5 years old".

"Maybe, when she grew up, she overthinks about it. Somewhere she is right, I shouldn't have left you."

"That time was different. Forget it."

"Okay, Tada," Shelly disconnected the call.

A year passed, they all forgot that 'Inder incident'. Lucky and Khwahish were sixteen years old. One day Khwahish asked her Momsy. "I wanna know your dreams, Momsy!" As if she would get all the answers instantly.

"I buried my all dreams woefully 1000ft under the ground, even if I set up a camp to dig to pull them out...it won't be

118

possible, that's impossible now. I can't get them back. So I don't want to share an impossible tale. They are all lost. You can go to sleep and don't overthink so much about your Momsy. I am fine," She smiled mysteriously.

"Okay!" Khwahish took her diary and started making her notes. She ignored her mother.

Barkha was thinking about her daughters that they both completed their schooling. And now they will have to step into the outer world. They will have to go outside of this house. Their entire world was their school, this house and me only. I know the value of higher studies. I shouldn't stop them from growing, especially Lucky, as she has potential, got good marks and secured number 1 ranking in the school.

She wanted to be a great fashion designer in the town with an international degree. She told her one day, she wanted to get enrolled in a foreign university. She deserves it, but she can't afford the fees.

Barkha got worried about arranging money for Lucky's higher education. Barkha thought to call Shelly to take permission to sell some part of the land they owned in the village to get money for her daughter's education. Being highly self-responsible, she didn't want to borrow money from friends or relatives or any financial help from Shelly's brother living in the USA. She didn't achieve great things in her life yet, however she knew her self-worth and the prestigious family she belonged to. She wanted to maintain those roots given by her parents and Grandma.

Lucky was a mature, sensible girl. She was fully aware of the world as she used to read the newspaper every day. She was practical in her life. Khwahish hated newspapers, and she was still unaware of the outside world, corruption, politics, evil and greed. Everything was so perfect in her dictionary. Everyone living outside of her house was like her family. She didn't even know how to deal with people, whom to trust and not. She was fragile and naïve. That's why her Momsy was still so protective of her. Even after her schooling, Khwahish's world belongs to her home only, nowhere else. She assumed Momsy wouldn't allow me because I didn't get good marks. Lucky was allowed now to attend her hobby classes like painting and cooking.

In the evening, Lucky served her mamma a cup of coffee with milk and 1spoon of sugar.

She observed that Barkha was in deep thought. She asked her mamma, "What are you thinking?"

"Nothing, Lucky, just thinking of selling our property in the village for all your further education."

Meanwhile, she served one black coffee without sugar to her adorable younger sister.

"Thank you, Babes!!" Khwahish replied quizzingly.

"Don't make a mockery of everything all the time, be serious. You are the dumbest." (Khwahish was childlike, never gets serious about anything).

"Momsy, ask Lucky why she is calling me the dumbest. Am I seriously one?"

"Lucky, don't call her the dumbest."

"Mama, her name is too long to pronounce."

"Okay, we will call her KOKO."

"Lol," She ignored Khwahish and continued talking to her mamma.

"Mamma, don't think about selling the land. At least I don't expect this from you. You are not a kid like that dumbest Khwahish. Maama, think wisely. The land in the village is a blessing from your Grandma. How would you even think that I will become successful in life after selling those blessings? Don't do this, mamma. Please. Act smartly." Lucky again continuously started talking about her dreams and future,

"I gave up on my dreams cause I woke up now. Mamma, I like my simple life. I am not that ambitious. I like colours, love spending my time doing paintings and cooking. I like to help you in the kitchen. I am still fine if I don't get enrolled in a foreign university. I will pursue my Graduation living in Ramgarh only. This town too has better universities. I love the comfortable life that you gave me. I have a roof, clear water to drink, clean and different clothes to wear, yum food to eat, what else do I need to live? I will become a full-time painter. And for that, I don't have to leave the house either. I can live with you forever without any regrets."

Listening to their conversation, Khwahish laughed out loud at Lucky, "What rubbish are you talking! What would you do for the whole day at home? We both are grown up now, and you would spend your whole day at home cooking food and painting in…this small house? Don't you want to be successful? Don't you want to own luxury goods? We can live like a fairy world. Everything around would be so classy and expensive. Numbers of servants, drivers. It will be so amazing. These feelings give me goosebumps.

Moreover, how long can Momsy do household chores and bear all the expenses alone for her daughters? It's our responsibility to look after her needs and fulfil this house's necessary basic things. She is our Momsy. She won't say anything to her daughters. It's all up to us to look after her now onwards," Khwahish said.

"Lol!! C'mon wake up, KOKO. The life you are talking about isn't possible in actual life for people like us. Look at our circumstances. Our mamma has been struggling hard in the Boutique for us. She needs us to be with her. Her actual happiness is to be with her daughters, not materialistic goods. We are simple people. The life you are talking about is not possible for people like us. We don't have enough sources

121

and higher contacts to approach. Moreover, we are girls, and we have limits. Wake up from your sweetest dreams. Dreams look good only in the movies and stories books. I, too, gave up on them. I can't let mamma sell that property for my Higher Education abroad. I can't leave this house and mamma. Apart from this, cooking and paintings are one of my personal favourite hobbies. I like to learn new recipes. I don't feel anything wrong pursuing my interests further, staying at home only. I love mamma. I can't leave her. I would give up on dreams," Lucky said.

Khwahish thought it was all rubbish.

"How one can stay home all the time? We already have been staying at home only since childhood. Doesn't she want to move outside and see the world? Doesn't she want to explore the entire world? And How can she be okay with it?" continued…"Momsy and Lucky think alike. That's why she always takes her favour. Lucky is probably not that motivated. Yet I am sorry, I am different from her? Even if I am right or wrong, I don't know anything yet as I am still naïve to judge her perception of life and dreams. I mean how one can't leave their comfort life and how long they can survive living in their comfort zone! After all, you live every day and die only once. You should make each day count, and I want everything from life. I can't give up on it. My dreams are like my unborn babies. I have to look after them, so they are so precious to give up for anyone. I don't know if I am right or wrong. I still dare to dream, and I promise to fight to fulfil my dreams and goals until my last breath. That's a Khwahish Promise, just wait and watch, my girls," Khwahish said in her cruel way.

"What would you do? We don't have enough sources and support. Hence I don't dare to dream. If I would dare or expect much from life, I will end up hurting myself later. I don't expect so much from my life. I like my comfortable life. Well, what do you want to become? What do you want to do in your life? What are your dreams?" Lucky asked.

Khwahish wanted to become an air hostess. Lucky and Barkha used to make fun out of her higher expectations from life. They both never paid enough attention to the words that came out of her mouth as Khwahish was an uninhibited girl. She had a light-hearted persona. She was a drama queen & ambitious soul. Yet, she takes her life at ease.

"Lol, Air Hostess! Do you even know how to spell Air Hostess! and how challenging the job is!" Lucky said, pulling her leg. She continued, "No one would be going to select you either. You would be rejected on the first attempt. Just look at your face, and look at your smile is like a devil," Lucky loved to tease her younger sister.

Whenever Lucky teases her younger one, she pretended like leaving her house forever.

"Momsy, ask her to stop teasing me, or I will leave this house forever." She mimics, carrying a trolley, leaving the house with a 30" family photo frame. (they clicked on her fifteenth birthday).

"Bye, I am going to leave all of you forever. I swear, I will never return. I swear, I will find my father and live with him. As I don't wanna live with both annoying ladies." After a few minutes, " I changed my mind. I will leave the house by Monday, wait and watch." Khwahish retorted aggressively.

Her childish acting makes her sister and Momsy laugh and love her more. What a girl she is! adorable. Everyone could wish to have a baby like her. Khwahish reminded Barkha of the Lil fairy.

"I knew it. Your MONDAY would never come!" Lucky said because once Khwahish told randomly that I have a Training held on by Monday next week.

"Momsy, please ask her. She again has started. Momsy, ask Lucky not to pull my legs, she can make fun of me, yet she doesn't have the right to make fun of my dreams and goals. Whenever I discuss anything about my career and lifestyle I wanna pursue further, she starts teasing me. She doesn't even know how valuable one's dreams are. I have been dying to fulfil my goals and dreams in their most extreme form. Instead of understanding it, she is making fun. She is my elder sibling, not an enemy. She should support me and keep her younger one motivated. Instead, she is procrastinating that we don't have a source, support, better schooling, higher degrees, etc. Momsy, I don't like these excuses. They are just excuses. If one dares to dream, they can fulfil it. I know it. I don't want to argue further on this matter."

Khwahish was the only one in the house who missed her father a lot. Living like a perfect family with a father under one roof was one of Khwahish's wishes. But she didn't know who her father was, yet she loved him a lot. She missed him, and she used to talk to him as if he lived with them and listened to her.

Chapter 23

A Dream to Fly

On, 11th January'2004

She saw one advertisement in the newspaper about training and selection for "Cabin Crew" held in the same town. After reading about it, she couldn't wait for a second. She wanted to talk about it, and she called her mother.

"Momsy, please come to me and see. I have something to show you."

"Yeah, tell me, what's the matter?"

She handed over the newspaper and asked her to read the given advertisement.

"Momsy, I so want to go for this. Please allow me. You don't know how much this means to me. All I need is your permission to go."

"The same town?" she asked.

"Yes, Yes, the same town. We need to go tomorrow only," she answered excitedly.

Khwahish discussed her ambition to her Momsy how much she was keen to pursue her career in this field. Her mother agreed to go along with her daughter for the interview. Khwahish was nervous. She wore a black T-shirt that her mother's friend had gifted her and blue denim jeans. It was her first denim jeans that she bought for herself. So she chose it to wear for the interview also. And she wore sports sneakers. She always loved to see her mother in cotton made decent sarees. Khwahish pulled out her favourite saree from the wardrobe for her Momsy. It was a maroon coloured cotton saree (*she even gave it the name "bedsheet"*) Barkha got herself ready. She was completely looking like a Queen. A natural beauty, she didn't need to put makeup on to look good. Her inner beauty was enough to give a glow to her face.

When she was all set to go and came to Khwahish, she kept staring at her mother without a blink of an eye, "Momsy, I wanna marry you." Her innocent heart meant by this that she wanted to be with Momsy forever. She didn't need anyone in her life other than her mother.

"Shut up, what nonsense!" Her mother laughed at her innocence.

They both headed for the interview. She was in the queue, standing behind six candidates, the interviewer called her name, and she moved towards them and sat in front of the interviewer. One beautiful, slim, well-groomed lady was taking the interview. Khwahish was just smiling to hide her nervousness, interviewer Ms Shikha asked, "Why are you smiling?"

She could only say, "Just like that." Ms Shikha continued asking for personal details, i.e. name, age, height, education qualifications, and family background. She answered all the questions carefully. The interviewer asked her one last question: what would you do if you were selected to serve as a cabin crew on a good salary package? She replied, " I will give it to my Momsy."

"Momsy?" She asked.

"Yes, to my beautiful Momsy," Khwahish explained, pointing towards her mother standing in the guardian queue.

Her interview was done, and she returned home with her Momsy.

One week later, she got an offer letter from the same airline where she was interviewed. She got selected, but their training fees were higher. "Lucky already denied to sell anything, somewhere she was right too, and Momsy didn't like to take out loans or any financial help. How would she arrange my money for the training?"

She didn't want to give this massive burden to Momsy; therefore, she hid the letter in a safe place, which her Momsy can never reach.

She decided to lie to her mother that she got selected for the airline training without paying any fees. Giving up on her dreams was not so easy for her.

The same day in the evening, Khwahish entered the kitchen first time, she opened a recipe book to prepare tea for her mother. It sounds a bit strange here as cooking was not her subject. A few minutes later, she called her Momsy to have a cup of tea. Her Momsy came downstairs and looked at her surprisingly "What is wrong with you, my doll! Am I watching a beautiful dream! or you are not well today!?" She called Lucky, "Look what's wrong with KOKO? She prepared TEA for us."

"Momsy, sugar ?"

"Just a single spoon," Lucky answered rudely.

"Momsy, actually I need something, I got selected, but my training has been held outside of this town. I need permission for that. Moreover, it's free of cost, we don't need to pay the fees. I swear I will work hard to make you proud. I promise it's a Khwahish Promise ." She was trying hard to convince her Momsy.

127

"Big No," She moved towards her room with her Tea. Barkha refused without any second thought. Barkha wasn't feeling good about the idea of sending her daughter away. Her instincts were not allowing as if there was something fishy. Khwahish avoids making eye contact when lying. During interacting with her Momsy, she avoids looking in her eyes. Barkha caught her because she was hiding something. She was young, beautiful, talented, yet not so mature like other girls of her age. Lucky and Khwahish, too, had argued and ended up deciding she will not be going anywhere and live with her mother only.

One month passed, she almost forgot her ambition as she knew whatever she would choose to do in her life, Momsy and Lucky would eventually refuse it. They both love being at home only, and they were content living with a few bucks. She was living with Lucky and her Momsy, but she stopped talking to them. One day at the breakfast table, she saw the colour of wine red, a thick magazine almost containing 15 pages. It was a free magazine that came along with the newspaper in the morning. She ignored it at first glance. Later she saw it again and picked it up to see, "What's this?" she murmured. She turned its front cover page, and she kept staring at it with her jaws open. She was stunned, like she saw some ghost. It was nothing like a ghost. It was beautiful, shining, marvellous, and a luxury sports car collection along with its complete buying information.

Khwahish and her family had a simple lifestyle. However, She wanted everything in her life. Her expectations were higher than others. She saw those cars in the pictures and felt thrilled, the same as she felt in her childhood when she was a newborn child. What if she got her favourite car someday. And gift herself a brand new luxury sports car at any cost. Seeing those cars, she couldn't restrict her desires. She wanted them badly. She started researching its prices and availability in her town. First, she thought that they all were only in the pictures, not in reality. Later she came to know that they were available outside, and people buy them to give them enough comfortable life in their physical world. She wanted the one at any cost.

Chapter 24

The Dumbest Girl

*M*onday, on 29th March 2004. She left her house, leaving a note behind, "Momsy, I can't live like this in a small house with availing basic life. I love my life, and I want to explore everything. I want to design my World, my lifestyle." Leaving a short note behind early in the morning, around 05:30 am, she left the house forever.

Reading Khwahish's note, Barkha thought she lost her daughter forever. She would never come home again, "This girl was just empty-headed, no one can help this girl, why can't she become polite and serious in her life like my elder daughter Lucky! Lucky and I denied her on choosing inappropriate desires. We used to restrict her all the time as her unwanted desires weren't appropriate. How come she thought that we were her enemy, we never restricted her to achieve big. We both knew how tough it was to survive in the outer world without any support. How can we protect such an unintelligent, stubborn girl?" She murmured. continued…
"Lucky had gone to one art gallery to visit an exhibition held for a few days in the same town only. She didn't want to disturb

Lucky by telling her about all this shit that her sister left the house without telling us the reason, as she would get affected by this and will come straight to me. She is my obedient kid, not rebellious." She didn't even want to put her energy to find her as she left without telling anyone. She left even after Barkha's selflessness protection, explanation and denial to not to go outside. "Should a mother die, protecting her children? What if a child becomes so rebellious and stubborn?" Barkha was annoyed with Khwahish's immature decision.

"We would have supported her if her reasons were pertinent. At least she should have shared it with us. What strongly made her think that she had to leave us like this? I don't know why this girl did this to us? Anyway, may God bless her." For a mother, it was an unbearable pain to accept, but Barkha's only bad habit was she never forgave people easily and their mistakes. The same reason she left her husband forever.

Now Khwahish needs lots of blessings. Khwahish was an unpredictable girl. No one can predict what was going on in her brain and what her expectations from life were. She didn't do hard work studying in her school to obtain higher marks. She was content with her minimum marks, as she knew life's practical knowledge and professional experience was always her top priority. We read theory in our schools, but our real-life starts after schooling. She knew the value of degrees and education, it's undoubtedly mandatory, but also, she was content with getting average marks. She used to defend herself when her marks were compared with Lucky, saying, "My Momsy never completed her schooling but she has far more experience of life than other working people." and maybe somewhere, she was right."

Khwahish had a childlike heart. She didn't know the reality of the outer world. She left the house thinking that everyone was good protective like her mother. She thought everyone had the same kind heart as she had. Standing under a bridge waiting for any help, she never imagined that she would have to leave her own house the way she used to pretend. Her real life's journey had started. Khwahish left the house, but she couldn't understand where to go now, whom to approach first? It was her first time, she walked without her Momsy, without approaching any unknown person, she called on the number given in her selection letter.

"May I speak to Ms Shikha?"

"Sure," A lady transferred her call to Ms Shikha.

"Hello?"

"Ma'am, Khwahish this side."

"Khwahish, who?"

"Ma'am, I am grateful, I got selected for the interview you had taken a few weeks ago, I want to attend its training programme, but I can't afford its fee. Can you offer me a scholarship?"

sounds amateur and nervous

"Excuse Me, I haven't recognized you yet, you can come to my office, and we don't provide scholarships."

"Ma'am, I want to, but I can't afford a ticket to Mumbai. If you can arrange one ticket for me, I would be highly obliged."

"Ticket! Can't you even afford a ticket?"

"Honestly, No. But surely, I will pay it back after getting a job."

"May I know your full name and from which place are you calling me?"

"Ma'am, This is Ms Khwahish, calling from my favourite Ramgarh."

Paused Ms Shikha put the receiver aside to think, "This girl asking me for help can't even afford to buy a ticket to come to my office. And the way she has been answering as if she is a princess of Ramgarh and ordering me to send her a 'Paper ticket'. Overconfident, but I want to meet this girl. She sounds amateur, but she has a zeal, an innocent as well, the way she asked for a scholarship and a ticket."

After few minutes of hold, she grabbed the receiver back. "Hello?"

"Yes, Ma'am."

"First you asked me for a scholarship, now you are asking me to send you a ticket. Do you even know how unprofessional it is? We don't book tickets for our candidates. You have to arrange enough funds for living here" Ms Shikha put the receiver aside again, started memorizing something.

"Where I interviewed a few weeks ago? Who is this girl? We don't make ticket booking for those candidates who want to come here for training. I can't go out of my procedure. She can get me into trouble, and an applicant never asks for ticket booking. There are so many selected candidates out there. What if they all started asking for free tickets?

Quite weird, this girl." She murmured. *She thought to disconnect the call, but she couldn't. continued…*

"Hello, I am sorry, you had to wait. But there is no direct flight available from your place to Mumbai. As far as I can tell, there is one seat available on a flight, and it's via Delhi, tomorrow at 10:00 am. I will inform my colleague Rohan. He will meet you at the Ramgarh Airport. He will arrange your travel for you to come to the Mumbai office. You will have to reach the airport around 08:00 am. My colleague will give you a paper ticket to board the flight."

"Thanks, ma'am."

She wore traditional salwar kameez, top to bottom fully covered with a blanket. She started walking to reach the airport as it was 5kms away from her recent destination. By hook or by crook, she decided that she won't go back home.

She reached the airport on foot. She slumbered that whole night in the female restroom at the airport.

She was struggling to come outside the ocean. A man dives into the ocean to save her life. He took her in his arms and came outside. Rather than being grateful to him, she shouted at him.

"Who are you? How dare you touch me!"

"Hi! I am Fitz. You were sinking. I had to dive into the deep ocean because I couldn't afford to see the dying beautiful girl in front of me. You could have died."

"I am Blugrey, a fairy mistakenly caught by fire in the forest. To protect my wings, I had to dive into the ocean, and I didn't know about its depth."

"The dumbest fairy I ever met."

"Don't act too friendly. It's too late. I must go to The Edenland."

"It's unsafe. Your wings already got half-burned."

She was upset, sitting at the beach with Fitz at midnight. As per fairy rules, she wasn't allowed to let any human love her outside of her Edenland, and whoever boy touches her first, she is bound to marry the guy to protect her beauty. Fitz touched her already while saving her life, and he was a human not belonging to her Edenland.

"Why would I even come on this land, among human beings, unnecessarily caught into the trouble."

"Why do you hate human beings?"

"Do I still have to answer?"

"What have I done?"

"Never say to anyone that you touched me while saving my life."

"Why?."

"Cause I don't want to marry outside of Edenland."

"How would you protect your beauty by hiding the truth?"

"I hate you."

"But I don't."

"Did you dive deliberately?"

"Just to save your life, as you were sinking."

"Can't marry you."

" I want to hug you, now." He couldn't, and he was not allowed, as it was against fairy rules.

"Why did you stop?"

"Cause I am not one from Edenland, and you hate me. She smiled, "I am already indebted as you saved my life, I would love to reciprocate. She gave him four magical coins:

One coin – Never let old

The second coin – Never let lose the spiritual path

Third Coin – Intelligence

Fourth Coin – unexpected Success and protection from evil

"When you'd become like water, pure and divine inside and outside, these coins would get double by itself. And if you become more powerful, then these four coins would be useless to you. Still, you have to protect the coins and spend them righteously to earn me. If they are eventually caught by negative energy, then you would get cursed and die a painful death."

"Blugrey, I have got a gift for you."

"Gift! You already protected my life. Well, what it is!"

"It's a word, an Italian word, Bei Capelli." He ran away

"But why did he say this?"

Fitz was running towards the forest. While running and before reaching the forest, he saw in every direction. In the east direction, there was a group of foolish people. In the west, several aged people were sitting under a tree, waiting to die. In the north, there was a group of the devil. In the south direction, a girl was praying to God to become successful.

He didn't go in any direction, as he wanted to hide the magical gold coin to keep them protected from negativity.

An old Greywitch living in the forest caught him with coins and learned about its magic power. Fitz didn't want to get cursed or let that coin be misused by that witch, as he loved Blugrey. Therefore, he ran towards the forest to find the safest place for the magical coins. He climbed a tree and kept four coins in a nest, and he slept in the shelter of the tree. The next day when he woke up, he saw each coin gave birth to another coin. he has to spend them righteously; otherwise, he would be cursed. He can't even let misuse it by that witch, who is standing under a tree waiting to kill him to get the coins. He throws the first coin in the west direction, the second in the north direction, the third in the east direction, and the last fourth in the south direction. He saw Blugrey coming towards him to kiss him to marry. *(It was a Dream, whenever Khwahish sleeps in anxiety, she sees a fairytale dream, maybe this is the way her great-grandma showers her blessings on her).*

The next day, she was all set to meet Rohan. He reached at the departure gate with a placard written: "Khwahish from her favourite Ramgarh." She collected the ticket from Rohan. She waited for her flight to Mumbai at the airport. Her first flight is about to come in a few hrs. Her heart was beating like a drum. She was nervous, as she didn't know the boarding procedures.

At the counter.

"Ma'am, Window seat or Aisle?"

"I don't know." Khwahish looked bewilderedly at her face.

"Are you travelling for the first time?"

"Yes, ma'am."

"Don't call me ma'am. I am Tish, and you can call me Tish. I assigned a window seat for you."

"Thank you, Tish."

"Your welcome. Enjoy your journey, ma'am."

Khwahish managed to board the flight. She was excited, nervous, and overwhelmed. "I shouldn't have left home. Am I a bad child? Would I go to hell? I took advantage of my Momsy's innocence. I can't even go back as I already borrowed a ticket. I never stepped out of my house without taking my Momsy's permission, but I left the house without asking her." Missing her Momsy, she started weeping like a newborn child. A flight attendant scrolling an airline service trolley on the walkway in the flight. She was wearing a red skirt, white shirt, red blazer with a nametag 'Kaycee' on it. She offered her a glass of water, "Ma'am, hope you're fine."

She got scared of the surprising arrival of a hostess, she nodded, as 'NO'.

"How can I go back? I want to be like her. Look at her uniform. I would love to give it the name "*The Uniform.*" The way she behaves to all the passengers with politesse, how well-groomed she is, and I love her decorum. I should keep my sentiment aside if I want to have a life like her. Moreover, I heard when emotions go higher, brainpower goes down." She whispered.

She was a bit loud while using hand gestures as she was upset, nervous, and overwhelmed. It was apparent to her as she was travelling for the first time by flight. She lost her senses & her palm was moving freely as if she was flying across the clouds, rather than in the flight. She couldn't control her movement, and her palm went straight to the cheek of a person sitting next to her. It was a slap.

"Excuse me! Ma'am, what are you doing? Could you please speak a bit slow? You are disturbing me."

Khwahish started to snivel. She couldn't even say the magic word "Sorry."

"Hi! I am Evam."

"Evam! What a name!" *In her babycry voice*

"Thanks, but I am sorry. I didn't mean to hurt you, and please calm down. I hate it when a girl cries."

"That's fine, EV."

"Now you crossed the line."

"What EV?"

"Not again. Nothing, just leave it." He just smiled, neglected her. He pulled out an inflight magazine distributed via airline from the front seatback pouch, started reading it as he loved gathering enough knowledge.

"Tell me, did I say something wrong?"

"My friends call me Evam only. I don't allow anyone to call me by this short name as I reserved EV wholeheartedly for someone special. Whenever I listen to EV from someone else, it makes my blood boil."

"Woah, you are an amazing guy. Whoever you're going to marry would be the luckiest one on the planet, I must say."

"Umm …I know. However, I haven't met anyone interesting yet."

At once, she slept on his shoulder and was drooling on his shirt. She was exhausted. It was manifest as she was going through a deep ocean of anxiety, as she didn't sleep for so long and was starving. Evam looked at her and smiled. Knowing her situation, he immediately called a flight attendant to wake her up. He didn't touch her. A gentleman in this new era."

The flight attendant came, "Sir, how may I help you?"

"Kaycee, right?"

"Yes Sir."

"Kaycee could you please make this lady sleep comfortably? She unknowingly slept on my shoulder. She is just my co-traveller," Evam said.

"Sure, Sir, I will do it. I am sorry for the inconvenience."

Khwahish was in her deep sleep. When she sleeps, she wakes up by herself only. No alarm can do this task in the world. The flight attendant shut the window shield, softly pushed her towards the window and gave her a travel neck pillow to support her sleep.

The flight was soaring high across clouds, leaving wind behind. The passenger felt tremors in the flight due to heavy pressure. Khwahish got up from the dream. The same dream she saw a night before at the restroom, "Who was that mysterious witch! Who was that boy Fitz! Where are those blessed five coins? Where am I?!" She opened the window shield. "Oh! it was just a dream. I don't know why I see fairy tales in my dreams." She softly slapped her head. And looked at the guy sitting next to her.

By looking at her co-passenger, "Ew, how did your shirt get dirty?" She asked, rubbing her eyes.

"A few minutes ago, you were drooling here. The flight attendant helped me."

"I am sorry."

"That's fine, fuggedaboudit."

"Can I call you Evam Bro?"

"Yes, you can."

"I need approval in writing."

"My words are everything."

"What a brilliant job the flight attendant is! What kindness they wear with their uniform! They deserve much respect and panegyrize."

"Yes, they do."

"What a voice you have, Evam Bro, I must say," She retaliated.

"Tell me something that I don't know."

"That you are handsome too."

"Lol, as you called me your brother. I would like to give you free advice, never get too attached or friendly with a stranger. Never trust anyone. I know your heart is made of pure gold as I can smell your innocence, the way you are & this world is not similar. Your innocence is your jewel. But it can be stolen, and you probably don't know more about what's going on in the world. Make a promise that you will never be too friendly like this to a random stranger ever in your life. We can't trust people so easily. None is worthy of being trusted. Moreover, your beauty and innocence can make any gentleman corrupt. You are like an exquisite flower. Believe me."

"I don't know as I never see myself in the mirror."

"Seriously!"

"Yeah, I profoundly consider the whole world as my home & the people residing on it are my family members & they would look after me the same way as a family member does, so I feel free, and yes I trust people, easily."

"The world is not like this, the way you think."

"Will make the world like this, the way I think."

"Lol, you are too innocent. May I know your name?"

"Khwahish."

"The beauty, the innocence, and the name. What a perfect born you are Khwahish. I need a promise that you will never talk to strangers."

"Yeah, that's a pinky promise Evam Bro. Never going to break it."

He wrote his number on a blank paper and gave her. "Whenever you need me, you can call me on the given number. I am just a call away. Consider me your big brother forever."

"No-No, please, I can't take your number."

"Take it, and you would need it."

"You are a true angel on the earth."

"I am a simple human being. I believe in simplicity."

"If you consider me your little sister, would you mind if I ask you something?"

"You can ask me anything, and I am all ears."

"I heard talking to you with a friend before boarding the plane, and you were mentioning a lot about a girl named Archie".

"Oh! Archie….., Archie and I are just good friends. She is beautiful, cute, brilliant, simple, independent, a well-raised perfect girl. I admire her the way she is. Nothing else."

"Bro, can this girl Archi call you EV?"

"I don't know, and I respect her the way she is."

"I want to know your answer."

"We have arrived in Delhi, and I have to go. TADA Khwahish."

Chapter 25

To Touch Horizon

A few hrs later, she touched down in Mumbai to reach the training centre where Ms Shikha, was waiting for her. She came outside at the arrival gate, saw one guy standing in the crowd holding a placard with the name written: "Ms Khwahish, from her favourite Ramgarh."

She moved closer towards the guy and asked him, "This is my name. Why are you standing here holding my name?"

He said, "Shikha Madam sent me to pick you up." She was on cloud 9th. She couldn't believe the good fortune she got today. She sat in the car, smiled and gazed outside of the car window, "Love you, Shikha Ma'am, I'm almost on my way to you." she whispered.

She reached the office. Ms Shikha came outside to receive her without wasting any time.

"So are you Ms Khwahish? from your favourite Ramgarh?"

"Yes, ma'am," She replied looking at the floor. She couldn't make eye contact as she knew that she came here leaving her house, without permission, without letting anyone know. To feel not confident was obvious because she chose the wrong way to pursue her dreams.

Ms Shikha kept staring at her for 60 seconds, "Okay, will continue our conversation inside my cabin. Let's go."

They both walked towards her cabin.

"Please have a seat."

"Thanks, ma'am."

She again stared at her for 2 minutes without saying a single word. Her gaze made Khwahish uncomfortable. She called the office boy to get her one glass of fresh orange juice and one plain veg sandwich.

"Ma'am, I don't eat sandwiches."

"Why? Due to its carbohydrates?"

"I prefer home-cooked hygiene food only."

"Look at yourself. How would you survive like this here?"

"No, ma'am, I don't need food. I need a scholarship for my cabin crew training, only."

She laughed out loud. "Ms Khwahish, there is nothing to do with food and scholarship. Just make yourself comfortable."

"Ma'am, I need to go to the restroom."

Ms Shikha explained to her the way which goes directly to the restroom.

Fifteen Minutes Later, Ms Shikha continued her conversation with Ms Khwahish.

"Where would you live here? Do you know anyone here? Any relatives or friends?"

She couldn't answer anything and started sobbing.

Ms Shikha passed her a packet of tissue to wipe her tears. "Use it as much as you can."

"Ma'am, thanks, but I am sorry."

"Are you fine?"

"I am sorry, Ma'am, I will stay in the office, keep myself starving, but I need the scholarship to complete my training successfully. I will return your full money, whatever you spent on me. I am ambitious but not greedy. I only want to get my training successfully done and want to work as a member of the Cabin Crew for Horizon."

"Khwahish, it is not as easy as you mentioned it, as I can see you have the zeal to work, but no other qualities can be seen. Do you know where you are sitting right now? It's Horizon. Let me explain to you in a quick way how it works. *First Step*, we select better, talented, well-groomed, good looking candidates, same as we selected you. *Second Step*, all interested candidates have to get their registration process first; by paying its full fees, there is no scope for the scholarship for anyone in Horizon. *Third Step*: After their registration procedure is done, we groom our candidates and train them in our dummy aircraft like a cabin Crew should work. *Fourth Step,* after completing the training session, senior members of Horizon will select the top five best performing candidates. All those five candidates have to face a semi-final interview Question & Answer round. *The fifth step*, their final interview, will be taken by Captain and Director of the Horizon Mr Singhal, by checking the presence of mind & level of IQ of the candidates. Then, they will select the best one out of five. One selected candidate would attend a training session held abroad **for Fifteen days. They finally get an opportunity and are appointed to work as a cabin crew member in our "Horizon Aircraft." It's a tough competition.** I hope you got the procedure. Working with an airline is a dream job. However, Initially, everyone comes here with more gusto, wealth, passion, and talent than you. They mostly leave for their home in mid of their training session. Candidates like you who have enough passion and successfully attend all training sessions eventually fail at the final interview. We send those candidates for another training to work at our ground office at the reservation desk. Yes, our fees are higher, but we create Brand."

Khwahish didn't reply. She kept staring at the floor. She remembered that girl who offered a glass of water a few hrs back on the flight. She forgot her face but still remembers the beautiful attire she wore. "The uniform," She murmured. She seems insane to Ms Shikha.

All of a sudden, Shikha stood up as Mr Singhal, director of Horizon, entered the room. He sent Shikha outside for 10 mins, and he interviewed Khwahish.

He continued, "I came here when you were crying. No-one cries out loud here like this. It's visible that you are not at the stage to handle our training or pursue your career with us. How does one amateur girl like you do this job? You are not made for this work. Moreover, we don't offer scholarships, as Ms Shikha already explained to you. Don't disturb Ms Shikha or pressure her for this again. You may leave now."

Khwahish didn't pay attention to what he was saying to her.

"The Uniform," she again murmured.

"Can't you listen? The dumbest girl, we are telling you to leave right now," He shouted.

"Sir, I have a selection letter," She tried to convince him.

"Congratulations!! It's not the final appointment letter to join aircraft as a cabin crew."

Putting her selection letter on the table, she tried to leave without saying anything.

"Wait," Mr Singhal stopped her.

She turned back, "What, Sir?"

"Can you work as an intern at our reservation dept? In the office without a salary?"

"Yes, I will. Thank you, sir, thank you so much." She left.

Ms Shikha standing outside, asked if she could share the room with her. Khwahish could do anything today to get an offer working for Horizon, an insane, passionate girl. Shikha offered her food and own flat in terms of returning her money after getting her job selection done as a permanent employee at Horizon.

"Why are you helping me?" Khwahish asked.

"I like your name."

Shikha laughed at Khwahish's stupid decision that she almost left her town. She will be working here and getting no salary in return.

"Ma'am, why are you laughing?"

"Nothing," She gave her a serene smile and wished her good luck for her bright future.

Khwahish wasn't worried about working without a salary. She knew that she would be gaining practical knowledge and better skills here without paying any fees from any institute by paying huge amounts of fees. She was observing people, the way they work, behave, speak to each other, the way they carry attire in the office. She was writing it in her notebook. She used to imitate them, the way people in Horizon used to communicate in the English language, to polish her communication skills at her rest time. Her goals and vision were all clear in her mind. She was a dreamer, ambitious & determined for achieving her goals. However, she was raised with principles & moral values. She was committed and loyal to her work. She wanted to achieve success with her honesty so that she could go back home someday and face her Momsy with an eye-contact.

She was so focused on her work. Her only distraction was her one colleague named Palache. Palache had a huge crush on Khwahish. He liked her because she was ambitious yet so beautiful. She was new in the office, just an intern but worked hard compared to others in the office. One day when he got to know that she is working without a salary, Khwahish didn't remain just her crush now. She became more respectful in his eyes. However, Few monsters in the office weren't happy with Khwahish. Maybe their reason was her talent, focus & dedication to work. She used to ignore her colleagues, be it male or female. She believed in minding her own business and not being involved in gossipings and dirty office politics. She knew the value of time, and she used to say, "Miles to go before I sleep." Such an attitude made her colleague feel weak and jealous. Few have evil eyes for her. She kept herself safe by praying all the time. She believed prayer has its limitless power. Her office colleague used to bully her and laugh at her the way she worked. They used to make fun of her clothes, her small-town accent. As she already faced the same in her school life, she never took all these so seriously. It didn't matter to her at all. None could distract her will as she believed in herself.

Whenever she got bullied in the office, she pictured her mother standing with her, trying to console and convince her that, "Something unsaid is far better than to get ourselves dirty in ugly fights and arguments. Moreover, there is no right or wrong, and it's all just a perception. Overthinking about negativity and toxic things won't affect them, but you. Remember, who deserves to be your good friend would never let you down. You are Queen, a winner, not a loser. People who bully others have their insecurity. Through their cheap stunt, they just satisfy their ego and nothing else. So don't give up. Fail, fail & rise like a phoenix from the ashes. Never give up, my girl."

Her female colleague Elisha knew that Palache had a crush on Khwahish. She always noticed Palache staring at Khwahish. But Khwahish always kept herself energetic and busy in her work only. She neither fought nor gave a damn to anyone in the office. Apart from her work, she was learning new words and its meaning from different languages. It was her baby step to speak multi-languages. So she started learning and understanding a few words. She kept using those words as if it was related to her mother tongue. Her goal was to make herself better than she was yesterday.

Moreover, she never wasted her valuable time criticizing other colleagues as many do during lunchtime in the lunchroom. Palache perceived her every day, "What does this girl want! look at her dedication without even getting a salary." The same day Palache took Khwahish's information from Ms Shikha on several special requests. Ms Shikha refused first, but later she gave him on the condition that he would never misuse it. Moreover, Palache was trustworthy in the eyes of Ms Shikha. He saved her from a big mess in the office. Otherwise, she would have never given the personal information on any condition to anyone. Since then, they hardly interact so much in the office except to pass a smile to each other. But they became good friends.

Fun Fact, Khwahish was an average student in her school. Her Momsy used to force her to a nearby school. She used to make several excuses to avoid her school and to stay home with Momsy. However, Khwahish maintained her 3D in professional life, i.e. dedication, discipline, and determination towards her work. At lunchtime, everyone used to go to the lunchroom to have their lunch, but Khwahish used to spend her time at her desk collecting knowledge from the computer screen. The technology, what proper use of it!

She usually spent her lunchtime reading books and finding new ones to enhance her skill. She knew it would be beneficial for her intelligence grooming. She was a different girl among all the staff members. One day everyone was in the lunchroom. Elisha saw that Khwahish wore a new wrist sports watch. She assumed that Palache only gifted her. Exasperated, Elisha, without any second thought, moved towards Khwahish and threw water all over her wristwatch. Khwahish remained calm and silent. She didn't say anything to anyone about the bad behaviour. However, Palache sneak-peeked at everything standing far away through the window.

The next day, Palache got a chance to talk to her, and he tried to give her a new wristwatch. Her mother raised a warrior, not a victim. It was against her principles, so she refused to take it. Every girl in the office wanted to go on a date with him. How dare she refuse to accept a gift from him? Hazel eyed, 6ft, athlete body, brown hair. Palache came to the office driving his red luxury car (beauty). Palache's ego bruised. Possible as he was a son of one of the top guns in the country. She was from a small town, a struggling newcomer, zero earnings, and such an attitude. Although, he appreciated her honesty. That was the day he decided he would marry Khwahish only. "That's my wife," He whispered.

Horizon works 24x7. This is what makes Horizon successful and different. On this matter, Khwahish was the first rule breaker in the office. None can make her go to the office on Saturday-Sunday. She loved to spend her weekends staying at home, listening to music, for her meditation and yoga. All those 90's released movies she had been watching these days. Few movies had so much violence and action, "I got scared, but the climax was good. Anyway, at least I got to know why Momsy didn't bother taking us to the cinema hall, or why she didn't buy Television for entertainment at our house. It seems like torture, but it wasn't her intention. It was just to keep her daughters disciplined. And to keep us away from all negativity, so what, if it was a part of the entertainment! That didn't matter to her. She didn't even bother to take us to the nice restaurants or cafes because she was worried that usually in cafes girls would come with boyfriends and in the family restaurants, we would see a family with father and ask her about our father and miss him. The reason she decided to keep us away from the outside world. Thank God she allowed us to step out for schooling. She gave her daughters a simple but rich life how we used to complain and hurt her, for not taking us to the cinema hall on weekends and so many other complaints. We made several mistakes living at home only, but she never complained about her daughters. Why are all moms like this? I miss you so much, Momsy, and you were always right. I am sorry. Please forgive your Koko. I want to come home."

Chapter 26

L'amour de ma vie

*T*ime passed, and it has been almost one year since she started working and learning without getting a salary. Still, no one nominated her to become a permanent employee in the office and could achieve the employee of the month title. She was unaware of politics & mind-games in the office that made people bad-mouth and negatively impacted, even after you are giving your best. However, she was never affected by it. It is okay. She was here to learn, and she knew that was a long way to go. "At least I got a chance to work with Horizon." She was not there to be just an employee of the month. That was just propaganda among colleagues. That was not an achievement.

When the title employee of the month was announced, Khwahish assumed she would become one with a permanent employee in the office, as she had been working as an intern. Unfortunately, it was still not on the list. Khwahish was standing right ahead of Ms Shikha and intensely scrutinised her abilities and underestimated that she was not doing well in the office somewhere. Maybe there was something that was still missing. Her internship was also almost over now, where was she making mistakes and lacking in her efforts that no one gave her a chance to prove her ability to work as a permanent employee in the office, "At least, I will start getting a salary, would save and would be able to afford fees for training as a cabin crew on my request, as well. It was like just an unplanned imagination that was going nowhere." Tears rolled down to her rosy cheeks, and she couldn't stay for so long among her colleagues who already weren't so much impressed by her. She felt uncomfortable, so she came outside of the office.

Palache wasn't in the office when employees of the month were announced, and he came late when it was almost over. Palache wasn't ambitious enough, and he had been working with Horizon only to keep himself away from his family, as he liked living independent.

His father was one of the successful businessmen in the textile industries and politicians of the country. The director of Horizon was a childhood friend of his father. Palache didn't come to the office riding a two-wheeler or driving a small car like his other colleagues used to. He used to go in his sporty luxury car. His car had gull-wing doors, a perfect shining red sports car, which normal people could only dream of, even to take a glance at such cars. Palache was a gold spoon, spoilt brat, maybe the reason his attitude was savage. As he entered the room, he looked for Khwahish, but she was not anywhere in the office. He asked the office boy about her.

"Did Khwahish come to the office today?" Palache asked the office boy.

"Yes, I saw her last time, wiping her tears. She was going towards the cafeteria, and she was looking disturbed."

"Can you please give me your Bike's key?" Palache asked the office boy.

"Excuse me, Sir!"

"Yes, you heard right, your bike key? my red beauty doesn't like narrow roads and slow speed."

"It's completely my pleasure, sir, and this is my bike key for you."

Palache was worried about her. She was in trauma; maybe she could think about ending her life. Somewhere, he knew that she left her house and needed emotional support. He searched for her, after searching for her in every possible place, finally, he saw the dumbest girl, wearing a white shirt, red knee-length skirt, black wedges, messy hair bun. She was sitting under a big tree at a lonely beach and was eating a giant pretzel inappropriately. Her eyes were staring at a wine-coloured magazine lying on a dirty floor. It got crushed into several pieces. She was smiling at the carcass of her dream. This girl seemed weird to Palache, and he came closer to her.

"Hey!! Khwahish, what are you doing here? And from where you got this? Horizon's Trainee uniform! Well, you are looking pretty," he was trying to make her smile.

"Who are you! Khwahish who!"

"Stop creating scenes. Are you sure! you seriously don't know who I am!"

"No,"..... and she got busy finishing her Pretzel.

"I am your colleague, and we have been working at the same office for almost one year."

"Colleague! Office! Which office? please go and stay away!"

"I guess you lost your mind." He picked one piece of carcass magazine lying on the floor and asked her, "What it was! Why did you destroy it! I know this belongs to you only. I caught you several times watching it."

"They are just ashes of my dreams," She felt desolate.

"It's completely fine not to be selected. If you have not been selected in one, destiny has a much bigger plan than you expected. So ignore being just a permanent employee or employee of the month title. Be concentrated on your work." It was the second time he gathered enough courage to talk to her.

Khwahish looked at him aggressively.

"What work! Do you know what I have been going through! I have a huge debt to pay to Ms Shikha. Ms Shikha has been bearing my living cost in Mumbai for a year. She is kind-hearted, she never asks about money, but I hardly admire it to be a burden on her. I have been working as an intern without getting any salary. I am afraid to say, Horizon just used me."

"Did they make any promise to get you promoted instantly while you were joining as an intern ?"

"No, I only assumed so, that seeing my hard work and dedication in the office, they will offer me a scholarship to take training for the cabin crew," She replied.

"Seriously!? What sort of girl are you!? Are you for real! Or mistakenly arrived here from another planet!? You solely sound like a joke to me. It's not a fairy tale. I must say that you are still not living in the real world, and you are living in the Elysian Fields. Do you even know? Or do you have any idea about it? How tough competition it is to be selected for a cabin crew through Horizon!? You should be grateful that Horizon gave you a chance to work as an intern. You are the only girl working as an intern. Otherwise, there was no possibility to get in Horizon as you did. That's only your fault, not theirs that you expected so much from them. You are so innocent to the world. Better you go back to your home. I don't even know why you are struggling! What you want to do in life! What was in that destroyed magazine! You are not a bold girl, and people might harm you."

"I don't have any idea what I have done. I don't have sufficient funds to get myself registered as a trainee of Cabin Crew in Horizon. I feel like I'm stuck in the middle of any roadway and can't even go home!"

"What's in your mind! Cabin Crew isn't a piece of cake. Working in the same aviation group which appointed you as an intern won't make you be one of them. Moreover, you are not even a permanent employee of Horizon."

"I want to go to my Momsy." She got up and ran, and she was stuck in the middle of the road where traffic took its place. She could have met an accident if Palache hadn't saved her from heavy traffic.

Palache wanted to lessen agitation. He started making funny faces to make Khwahish laugh. He made comic faces and mimicked in front of Khwahish. He just wanted to give her a ray of happiness as she was too upset.

"Lol, I am sorry for being rude to you. The way you motivated me, I should be grateful. Well, quite a nice try to impress a girl, my buoy," Khwahish said quizzingly.

"Buoy! You are funny. I always thought that you are an introverted girl, but you are not."

"Yes, I am not!"

"Hey! I have got a gift for you but first want to see your smile like flower blossomings."

"Thanks, but I can't take anything from a stranger."

"Stranger!" He looked at her without a blink of an eye.

"Stop looking at me like this. Okay, I will take the gift from you."

"He handed her one gift-wrapped box."

"What's inside?"

"La vie est belle."

"La vie est belle? What does it mean?"

"Find it on your own." Palache smiled at her mysteriously.

"I am grateful for this, but I have nothing to reciprocate on behalf of this."

"That's fine, can you spend your whole life with me? If yes, then tell me your favourite colour."

"That's serendipitous."

"Do you have a Boyfriend?" Palache asked.

"Exaggerated, no car, no date. I was watching a lot of movies last week. So don't mind, just ignore my humour."

"I don't mind because I don't have a mind."

"You sound nervous."

"Yes, your beauty made me so. Why did you say no car, no date? That wine-coloured magazine too designed with many luxury car collections. I wanted to steal it. Why did you destroy it? I got it, and the mystery has been resolved now. I wondered what made you so passionate about your dreams, so this is what keeps you on your toe? This is why you have been working so hard? First, to become an Air Hostess, and second, to get that your dream Car, right?"

"I don't know." She looked at the ground, replied softly.

"But I know that you want to own one out of that magazine. Isn't it?"

"Please stop pursuing PhD in Khwahish. I am sure you won't graduate. Anyway, I have to leave as my Momsy doesn't like talking to strangers, especially to boys."

"Alright, can I have your number?"

"Excuse Me!"

"Yes, you heard right."

"Big No," She retorted, making an O-face, rolling her eyes.

"No problem, I already have it," he murmured, looking at the floor."

"What!"

"nothing, ……… Momsy!?" Palache asked her.

"Yeah, my Momsy."

"You were talking about your mother, right?"

"Yeah, talking about my Momsy," she replied.

"You are the dumbest one, seriously, who calls their mamma a Momsy. It's uncommon to me. She is mamma, try to say maa…maa, mamma, not Momsy," Palache tried to correct her.

"M…..MO…MSY…..It would definitely sound fake to you that I can speak everything, yet, I can't speak this word you are trying to correct me with. My Momsy corrected me 1000 times, and I can't help with it. None can. Because it has been since my birth, I can say birth defect. She is my Momsy only. She doesn't have any problems."

"You just pretend to be innocent, naïve but you are not in actual"

"Would you please, stop finding topics to talk to me"

Meanwhile, Khwahish gazed at a lizard on the wall and started screaming like a kid saying "Fish-Fish."

"ROTFL, Fish!? That's a Lizard. Whatta character she is. I am falling head over heels for her," Palache whispered.

"Hey, did you say something?" she asked.

"Did you hear something?" He replied.

"Not yet….nothing," she blushed.

"Why did you leave her, can I ask?"

"My Momsy was working and struggling hard to raise her kids, I mean to my elder sis and me. Yet, I am a selfish girl. I feel suffocated living an ordinary life, another birth defect. I want to make a better world for myself. I had to leave the house because she never allowed me to relocate with her approval."

"You love your Momsy a lot, no?

She smiled and remained silent, and she didn't answer.

"Your loving, adorable Momsy loves you more than Lucky. And beyond anyone in this world," He winked and left.

"How did he know that my sis name is Lucky?! He is just a mischief-maker, nothing else. I hate boys. He spoiled my time. Anyway, I should stop overthinking about him and should head towards my room," She murmured.

She was slightly upset because after giving her dedicated hours to work in the office, there was still no hope of being a permanent employee in the office & not being selected for an employee of the month. How tough working life is. She was upset, "What's going on in my life! Why and what I am doing here! Lord! Gimme a ray of hope! I left my house to give wings to my career, but I lost everything. One shouldn't leave home as I did." She wasn't able to sleep because it was almost a year, she was struggling without major support, it was apparent to her to miss her family.

Khwahish sent almost 2000 text emails (with one msg "sorry"), and made 1000 unanswered calls to her Momsy.

"Have I lost my Momsy's love forever?" Keeping her finger crossed, she tried her fate 1001 times.

"Hello!" Finally, the call was answered by Lucky.

"Hello, Lucky! Please don't disconnect the call. I know I made mistakes, I hurt Momsy, please ask her to forgive me, and call me home, I want to come back. You were right, Lucky. Materialism has nothing to do with happiness. I lost my inner peace," She started crying over the call.

"Khwahish! How are you! I am so glad that you called us." Lucky was glad, but more she was surprised

"I have been living in Mumbai for one year for my career. How are you and Momsy at home? I left home without informing her. I know I did wrong. Despite all my efforts, I have not been able to get success. I miss Momsy a lot. Is she still mad at me? Now I know her restrictions over us were to save our lives. She was saving us from all the negative aspects and people. We used to blame and complain to her most of the time in our childhood. But she was always right at her end. Being a single mother, she did great for her children. I have realized her love and care behind her restrictions. I want to talk to her now as I feel like I am depressed. I feel empty without her. I miss her badly. Can you ask her to talk to me? Just once."

"I am sorry, Khwahish, but she doesn't want to talk to you, she almost forgot you, like our father," Lucky said.

"Don't say this, Lucky, please ask her to restrict me, discipline me once again, call me home, tease me as you both used to do with me, as I can't live without both of you. Please ask Momsy to pick the telephone in her room. I know it's a two-way connection. We can talk together. I know I half spoiled my life unknowingly. I just want to hear her voice, don't worry, I will keep silent on call, and after listening to her voice, I will disconnect the call."

"Just Relax, let me try."

"Mamma, please pick up the call in your room. It's an urgent call for you." she spoke in a loud tone.

Barkha picked up the receiver.

"Hello! Hello! (pause for two sec.) KOKO! my doll. Are you fine?"

"Momsy! How did you know that this was me on the call? Moreover, I and Lucky, both were silent."

"You will get to know the beauty of motherhood when you become a mother."

"Momsy, please forgive me," she cried her eyes out.

"I already forgave you. A mother can never remain angry with her kids," Barkha replied.

"I made a major mistake, but how did you forgive me so easily?" Khwahish asked.

"That's the beauty of a mother's kind heart," she replied.

"Momsy, I want to confess something. I left home because I can't live without achieving my dreams. I felt suffocated in a mediocre life. I have been working with Shikha ma'am. You met her on the day of my interview. My work is at the reservation desk in her office. I am working as an intern. Shikha Ma'am is so kind-hearted. She arranged my living and food here, but I have not been earning a handsome package. I can say I'm getting nothing, but I have been learning a lot about my work here."

"I know that Ms Shikha helped you, she was worried about me, so she called me on the same day when you reached her office. Being a mother, I had gut feelings that wherever my daughter is, she would be fine. She keeps me updated about you and your friend. What's his name, Lucky please remind me. I forgot." They both were pulling her younger one's leg.

"Palache! How did you know about him? Tell me, Momsy and you, Lucky. He is just my colleague. Not even friends. I have been keeping myself busy with work here. I did not go outside with friends for parties and clubs."

"He comes every Sunday to our house to meet me and to look after me. He adores you secretly. He knows that you are immature and stubborn and won't come here without achieving your goals. He comes here every Sunday to meet me in his car. I have never seen such a sporty car in my life. I can say, Humanity is still alive, my child."

"I am sorry, Momsy. I didn't know that my true happiness is being with you, not materialistic or luxury things. I will leave this job and come straight to you by tomorrow."

And she hung up the call without listening further.

Chapter 27

Rang a Bell

*T*he next day in the office, the Director of Horizon, Mr Singhal, called Khwahish in his cabin and asked her if she was interested in attending training sessions for cabin crew. If she is interested, she can enrol herself to participate. She kept looking at him, "Sir, I think a minute ago you cracked a joke, or you called a wrong candidate. I didn't pay any fees yet."

"How many girls are working here with the name Khwahish and have blonde hair? I called the right name."

"But Sir, what about my fees?"

"We will make all the arrangements for you, don't worry."

She was looking at him with her eyes wide open and a big smile on her face. She was overwhelmed and wanted to pinch herself, as it was just a miracle for her. A day ago, she almost lost all hope, and she had been working here without a salary. She was behaving as if she had lost everything. She got the biggest news today. It's visible that Mother's prayer has its special power. she managed her joyful emotion and could only say, "Thank you Sir, thank you so much."

"There is one sacrifice you will have to make."

"What, Sir? Anything for this work."

"You have beautiful features, but your knee-length hair won't go with this job. You have to get them shorter."

"Sir! I wil..l……" *paused*… first she paid attention to his words…then …. "bei capelli" she whispered.

"Excuse me!"

"Sir, My hair is my pride, dignity and wisdom, I won't get them shorter to get a job."

The interviewer smiled, "What a presence of mind, Khwahish. Be Ready to Fly High."

In the evening, she called Barkha and told her about her training that she just got selected for fifteen days of training held in Kuala-Lumpur. If she gets selected, she will be appointed as a cabin crew member and stay there for almost one or two years.

"This is a great opportunity. Please allow me to go," She was convincing her Momsy to take authentic permission this time.

"That's big news, my girl. Congratulations, my doll, you already made me proud!!" Barkha gave her permission for Malaysia. She flies towards her dreams and loses almost all connection to family. She calls like once in two-three months, No everyday calls, no updates, nothing. If Barkha calls her, it remains unanswered from Khwahish, so she hardly calls her. "Girls of her age enjoying life with parents at home, but this girl Khwahish is a rebel, working just to get her favourite luxury car, selfish girl, too much dedication for a silly materialistic thing, isn't it foolish? Anyway, May god protects her. I gave up on this girl."

Barkha missing her husband Inder today, "How my life would have become easier if this man were compatible with me! Even my children don't give me enough time. What sort of life I have been living! Even Inder didn't try to contact me after that one worst incident. Why has God chosen me for this hard life!'"

Six months later, on 14th July 2007

The doorbell rang.

She opened the door and saw it was a delivery guy ringing the doorbell continuously. He handed over a bunch of 365 White Roses Bouquet, elegantly tied with Magenta pink Paper Ribbon.

"Wow! That's pretty! Beautiful roses! Who sent this?" she asked the delivery boy.

He smiled and just replied., "The sender refused to reveal the identity. I am sorry, ma'am."

"A crazy thing happened to me. Lucky, look! What a beautiful bouquet! I got it on my birthday."

"WOW!! That's so beautiful! Who sent this?" Lucky asked curiously.

"I don't know, he refused to reveal identity. The delivery guy apologised and left. Anyway, forget it. Let's celebrate my birthday with dark hot chocolate. I will prepare for you. I like to celebrate my birthday simple. I am not an introvert, but I like to stay home with kids."

"Oh, Mamma, you are such a darling," Lucky gave her mamma a warm hug.

"Okay! Now, will you please stop buttering me like Khwahish? This is what she does when she wants something from me. I miss her so much."

Chapter 28

A Missing News

On 16th July 2007, Barkha was sitting in the garden of her house alone, and she missed her mother and her younger one, her heart monster Khwahish. At that exact moment, her mobile phone rang.

"Hello, what are you doing?" It was her Maa's voice.

"I started working for one NGO here. Therefore I couldn't make calls to all of you, but why didn't you call me for so long? May I know the reason?"

"Nothing."

"What I have been listening about, Khwahish? She left the house!"

She neglected Shelley's word, "Maa, what perfect timing! I am in the garden, and I have been thinking about you only," she was trying to reduce the anxiety of her mother.

"Yes, I was missing you too, but I am mad at you."

"For what, Maa! What did I do?"

"Don't act smart. What did I hear about Khawahish from Lucky?"

"What, Maa?"

"Khwahish left the house without telling anyone in the house, and you didn't call me to let me know about it! I am her Granny, as well! Lucky told me you never even informed her, too, primarily. She has not been living with her mother and sister for almost one year. It's a long time to stay away without making any contact with loved ones. And no one informed me about her. Where is my Khwahish?"

"Maa, it's a long story, all sorted out. You did a lot for all of us. I didn't want to hurt you by telling Khwahish that she left the house for her career without telling any of us. You know Khwahish, how stubborn and selfish a soul since birth. No one can divert her mind when she decides to do something, so please forgive me and don't get mad at me. She is in Malaysia, and it's the safest country. She is perfectly fine and doing well, Maa. There is nothing to be worried about. I have been regularly keeping in touch with her."

"What's her phone number? Do I deserve to take her number?" Shelly asked.

And then Shelly hung up the call fiercely.

* * *

On 18th March 2008

At 06:00 am, early in the morning, Lucky woke up for her meditation.

Every morning after her yoga and meditation, she prepared coffee and breakfast for herself and her mother, then she used to wake her mother up. Barkha also maintained the same routine to look at Lucky's face first in the morning right after waking up. And then they both used to have breakfast together while reading the newspaper and discussing all the news that's going on these days outside in the world. This was an essential part of their everyday's routine.

As per routine, Lucky woke up and prepared coffee and breakfast for herself and her mother in the kitchen.

She entered her mother's room, adjoined to her room. She noticed that her mother was asleep. She touched her. She had a slight fever. So Lucky didn't feel appropriate to wake her up. Therefore, she let her sleep.

At the coffee table, she picked up the newspaper and started reading it. She was reading and turning pages one by one. There was news of politicians, accidents, and other incidents going on in the town and country. She loved reading. And kept turning pages one by one and reached at the end of the newspaper. She gazed at one news in astonishment, which said, "A Flight Disappeared."

Lucky tried to ignore the news. She got up and pretended as if she didn't read anything in the newspaper. She started walking. She didn't even know what she was doing. She went upstairs and then came downstairs. She went to her mother's room to check on her fever and body temperature. She was trying to wake her up. She wanted to wake her up, although she didn't. She was active physically, but her mind was stuck on that news she read at the coffee table.

"Which airline is missing? I have no courage to read the complete details of this news. Dammit!! What a dark day it could be."

Without reading anything, she hid the newspaper. She didn't want her mother to see it.

She saw her mamma at the stairs, coming towards her.

She asked, "Lucky, what's going on! Why didn't you wake me up in the morning and what's in your hand! What are you hiding!"

"Mamma, relax, pull yourself together. Mamma, you have a slight fever. I didn't feel pertinent to wake you up in the morning. At 6:15, I came to your room and tried to wake you up. However, you were looking pulchritudinous while sleeping, so I didn't want to make a mess."

"C'mon, Lucky. I am not a 5-year-old girl. Tell me, what are you hiding? What's in your hand?"

"Mama, there is news about a missing flight. I checked its flight no. It is the same Airline Khwahish is working for," Lucky said.

Barkha slapped Lucky.

"Just think and recheck the news. You are talking about your younger sister. Who is not living with us and working hard on her own. She is an independent, intelligent & self-made girl. You shouldn't talk about her like this. She is fine, and I know she is fine. Get me that newspaper."

"Mamma, I almost destroyed it."

"Let me talk to her office… to her boss," Barkha said.

She took her phone, trying to contact her at the regional office. She tried to contact every single person she knew from her office, but no one was answering.

In the evening, around 6 pm, she got a call from Ms Shikha. Barkha picked up quickly and burst out, "Ms Shikha, I want to know about Khwahish. Her number is out of reach. I tried to call her office and colleagues. But no one picked up the calls. Lucky told me about one news… that…I can't even say or think."

"Ma'am, Lucky was right. Khwahish's flight has been missing since last night. We don't have confirmed news. We don't know what happened to that aircraft, and we lost all our connections last night. That's it. We don't know much about it. We are investigating and trying our best to contact them. And will get back to you with the latest information about it as soon as we get any updates. We all are praying that Khwahish and all passengers are fine and they all reach their home safely. We are hoping the aircraft should be fine. We are optimistic."

Barkha could feel the voice sobbing from the other side of her phone as while consoling Barkha, Shikha couldn't control her emotions and started crying over the call.

"Please transfer my call to Lucky. I want to talk to her," Shikha said.

"Lucky, Ms Shikha wants to talk to you."

"Hello, Shikha ma'am, what's wrong with that Aircraft? I saw that news in the morning but couldn't hide it from my mamma for so long. Where is my sister? We had a word with her the day before yesterday. She promised me that she would come back to us soon and we would live together. Last evening at 11:25 pm, we lost contact with her, her phone was switched off, did you talk to her? What was she saying? Did she ask about mamma and me? If you can contact her, please tell her that Lucky and mamma will never tease her. Just ask her to come back. Please," Lucky too couldn't hide her mournful emotions.``

"Just calm down, Lucky, you are a sensible girl, don't lose your hope like this. You have to look after your mama, for Khwahish's sake. We all are trying our best to reach them. And hopefully will contact them by the end of the day. I am just keeping my fingers crossed. We are trying our best. But we still haven't made any contact with the aircraft. As soon as we get connected to them, I will ask Khwahish to contact you directly." Shikha tried to console them. Then she disconnected the call.

It's been a week. Lucky and Barkha were waiting for Khwahish to call them. Still no positive news about her aircraft. Barkha had an anxiety attack, as she couldn't bear this pain. She couldn't even cry, and she fainted in shock.

Lucky rushed over to get her mother. Lucky took her to the room and let her sleep. She started living as a depressed person. Being depressed, she stopped eating food, not even a single piece of bread or a sip of water. Khwahish's family were in huge shock. Especially Barkha, she loved her younger daughter but couldn't express her true feelings ever. She always pretends like she loves Lucky more than Khwahish as her younger one was too rebellious. She never listened to anyone. She was like a free spirit. She was such an adorable child. "When will I see her next!" And now she realized how she loved her younger one more than her life. She couldn't get over this malign truth. She stopped talking. She used to whisper only a single word, "KOKO."

A month passed, and there was no improvement seen in Barkha's condition and no news from the missing aircraft.

Barkha's mobile phone rang. She picked up and tried to speak—the call from the USA.

"Maa," she managed to say this and started crying out loud. She cried out loud like this for the first time after she heard Khwahish's missing news.

"Yes, honey, cry as much as you can. Won't stop you today. I heard from our neighbour that Lucky and you both have been skipping your meals! Not living life as you used to live! No cleaning, nothing like before! You don't even change your clothes! How would you live like this! It's almost been one month. You both almost forgot to live your life, even your basic routine. At least maintain proper hygiene, keep our house clean, and have your meal on time. How would you both sustain like this! At least think about Lucky," Shelly tried to console with her gloomy voice.

"Please give my daughter back. My Grandmother used to tell magic stories. Is there any magic in real life also to get my daughter back? I don't know, maa, I can't get over this bitter truth. This girl Khwahish was different from all other girls out there. If she decided to achieve something, she wouldn't stop until she succeeds. She is a stubborn hearted

169

girl. How often I taught her to behave like a mature girl, a sincere girl and avoid taking such a risky job. She used to say, "Momsy life is a risk itself. Risk is everywhere, don't run away from risk."

"She didn't even think about her Momsy. How would I live without her! She chose struggles for herself. Being too dedicated towards work wasn't necessary in her case. She could have lived with us like Lucky. My Lucky, my sincere, obedient kid, has also been living in her home without any complaint. We lost her Maa. We completely lost her. Could you please give me my doll back? I didn't know, but I loved her so much. I want to hug her hard and tell her how much I love her, how much I miss her sweet voice. She couldn't even speak "mamma" like Lucky, like all other children. My younger one was truly blessed. How can she die at this age? This is not her age to leave the world Maa."

Barkha poured her unbearable pain into words for the first time after her daughter's missing news.

Shelly disconnected the call. During their conversation, she, too, lost her emotions. It was a dark day for the entire family. They all accepted this malign truth about Khwahish. Time passed, and they all got back to their routine life.

* * *

On 14th July 2011,

Her doorbell rang

"Lucky, please open the door. Please check who is there?"

"Mummy, I have urgent work to submit. I have been working on my project. Please go and check," Lucky replied, unmannerly.

Barkha walked towards the main door. Meanwhile, the doorbell was ringing continuously. "Wait, coming. Just wait for a second. Who is ringing the doorbell repeatedly?" She yelled.

She opened the door and saw it was a delivery guy ringing the doorbell continuously. He handed over one bouquet, and it had 365 roses. With a note tagged – *'Happy Birthday, I love you so much.'* And one smiley emoticon was on the gift card.

She had been getting the same bouquet on her birthday without knowing who sent it to her, "Who sent this!" She asked the delivery boy once again.

And like always, he just replied., "They refused to reveal their identity. I am sorry, ma'am."

"I don't know who sends me a bouquet on my birthday at the same time without fail. I am not that popular. I am an ordinary woman."

Ten minutes later, the doorbell rang once again.

"Now, who is again at this time? It's 2:00 pm. It is not the time for the milkman and the newspaper's delivery time. Now, who is this?"

She rolled her eyes in exasperation and opened the door in annoyance.

"Who is this? Why are you annoying me?" she murmured while opening the door in bitterness and looked outside. Dumbstruck, Brakha kept staring.

"Momsy."

Someone was calling her name. The name she loved the most to be called but never pretended. The name that made her forget the entire world.

"Momsy."

She couldn't believe the gift she got today. Almighty blessed her once again.

On her 45th Birthday, Khwahish returned to her home to meet her Mother. She was wearing her "The Uniform", navy blue coloured knee-length skirt, light grey shirt, a navy-blue blazer, a sky-blue polka-dotted scarf wrapped around her neck and black 6" high heels. She was looking like a perfect Boss in that attire.

She gave her mother a warm hug. They both had mixed emotions, joy and sorrow.

"Khwahish, my daughter. Where have you been! No calls!…nothing…and no news about you!. We thought you left us forever," she couldn't control her emotions and started crying, cuddling her daughter Khwahish.

Without saying anything, Khwahish kept staring at her Momsy. Her face was like a wet weekend.

Tears run down her cheeks while handing over one box to her Momsy.

"What happened to that Aircraft!"

"A miracle."

"Miracle! Are you fine, KOKO? I want to know everything about what happened to you."

"Momsy, nothing was serious, forget it, we had lost connection with the ground staff due to bad weather, we had to land the plane at another airport, and by God's grace, we all were safe. We all waited to get further permission from the higher authority to fly. As we landed unexpectedly, its formalities took time. The entire team in aviation was extremely helpful."

"Why the news didn't appear in the newspaper?"

"Because some greedy media made things ugly deliberately to get few bucks, it wasn't like as it seemed to all of you."

"Hey! why didn't Ms Shikha inform me about this?"

"I am afraid I refused as I wanted to give you a surprise visit. Will you please stop asking questions and accept it," and she gave her one Gift Box wrapped around with golden glitter paper and tied with a beautiful bow tie red ribbon packaging.

"What is this box for! What is inside? I can't take it from you, and I don't need it."

"You ask a lot of questions, Momsy. You are still the same as an emotional queen. Now, will you please open it without asking a lot of questions and creating a scene, Please?"

"Okay", She unwrapped the box and saw it contained one handwritten note on the top, "If my coffin would have come today instead of me, these are the gifts I had prepared for all my favourite people."

She saw the box packed with five more tiny boxes. She picked one by one and opened it. Each gift box was a "Message" written on paper.

To Granny – 7 Kisses.

To Lucky – Thank you for looking after Momsy in my absence.

To Palache – Turquoise (the colour I loved the most).

To FATHER – Thank you for depositing my fees in Horizon.

To Momsy – Happy Birthday to you. Thanks for receiving a white rose bouquet every year on your birthday. I know you don't accept unknown things yet. Somewhere I knew you would never refuse white roses. I am grateful, Momsy. You are the best.

She gave another tiny box for Momsy on her Birthday. This box had one KEY, wrapped with a piece of paper, a story written on it. One nightingale gave birth to two cute little birds. One little nightingale flew away to see the world. The bird returned to her mother nightingale, poured her heart out and shared her experiences. The little one could only manage to say, I roamed across and flew around the world with my wings. I saw each corner of the world, sky to Beaches, North to South, East to West. And in the end, I got your Nest, a peaceful dream house 'Ashiana' *is the best.*

"Let's go to live together."

* * *

I dedicate this book to my parents because they are the only ones who gave me this beautiful life.

In our busy schedules and race of life, we forget that whatever we become and achieve in our lives, direct or indirect parents are always the reason for our success.

This book is for all dreamers. While achieving our goals, we overlook parents' care.

They are the only ones on this earth who never reject their kids come rain or shine we are going through. They are true wealth and strength. Hence never underestimate your parents and their sacrifices. Whatever they are and doing for you, be always grateful for them.

Right after reading this book, pick up your phone, make a call to your parents, say THANK YOU.

___KC

Some birds chirp

(Fiction, short stories)

Dedicated to a Pigeon (DOST) & a Lizard (A Fish)

Melted with a Kiss

*S*he was waiting for a friend with a colleague standing under a bridge. When a car came, she sat in the car with her colleague. Something there in the air was disturbing her. The fragrance of expensive perfume insisted on seeing someone next to the driver seat. She tilts her face to look at him and gets mesmerised. She felt as if watching a prince character came out of her comic book, from her fairy tales. "Such a boy even exists?" She whispered.

She was from a different country and came for the research. As she was ambitious and dedicated to work, she forgot about the boy after reaching the research centre.

But the boy fell in love when he saw her for the first time, standing under a bridge.

"Woah, I believe in love at first sight. She will be my wife." *whispered*

Her colleague with whom she came here listened to what the boy said, "She already rejected 999 boys without even knowing about them," She intervened.

He: Don't worry! I won't let any 1001 come into her life. She will be mine. Wait and watch.

The next day he came in his car and took her to the nearest cafeteria.

He: What would you like to order?

She: Ice tea without syrup

He: Would you mind if I order a cappuccino with four spoons of sugar?

She: No! Why would I?

He: Are you single?

She: No. I am committed to my dreams.

He: What can make you accept my proposal?

Her Hiccups started

She: Don't waste time.

He: Nothing is impossible for you.

She: Still NO

She bruised "A spoiled Brat" ego. Now he wants her by hook or by crook. "I want this girl." He had been thinking the whole night about her. The next day he got up to drop her at work. He rang her house doorbell. As she opened the door, he kissed her passionately without a second thought. (Counterattack). She always wanted the first kiss in front of Jesus Christ at the time of her marriage only. The moment he kissed her, she closed her eyes to imagine as if she was standing in the church in front of Jesus Christ. That day she got unofficially married to him. A divine kiss melted a stone-hearted and made her be with him for a lifetime as she too likes him. No 1001 could dare to come into her life now.

Ocean Blue Eyes

*H*e was staring at her pic for so long.
Can you envision what I am thinking? He said
She: What?

He: I want to swim in your ocean blue eyes.

She: I appreciate, but..

He: But what?

She: But my picture was filtered, Bro!

He: Bro!

She: Yeah! Our age is to study, to achieve goals, to make our parents proud. Stop wasting adolescence swimming in one's ocean blue eyes. Get up and Go!

He Left

Mango Juice in the wine glass

*S*he came home, sat on a dining chair, called her driver and asked to get red wine while coming home. Her sister comes to her from the kitchen.

Sis: What's the matter?

She: Nothing.

Sis: Then why you asked to get red wine?

She: Because I want to, simple.

Sis: You think I am a fool? I have been with you since your childhood. Tell me what's wrong.

She: I already told you.

Sis: As far as I know you. You are health conscious. If you are craving foods that you don't like, i.e., soft drinks, packaged food, which means you are hurt for some reason and want to harm yourself cause you can't say to anyone. I am all ears, tell me.

She: Woah! That's perfect. How you've known me?

Sis: Because I don't just pretend, I care for you.

She: I got rejected in an interview.

Sis: You are not born to work 9-5. You could lead. Why choose to work under anyone other than you? It's like you want to go to the moon but work on the farm. To reach the moon, work in the right direction. You have always chosen the right intention and dreams, but in the wrong direction with the wrong ones. The reason you failed.

She: So, I stop harming myself?

Sis: Obviously yes!

She: What in beverage then?

Sis: Your favourite Mango Juice in the wine glass.

My First Pizza

I never disrespected food, but I was living on water, fruits, salads & soup. After completing high - school, I eliminated spices, oil, food and grains from my diet. (I made my diet as I wanted to look fit. And teens ego wasn't ready to listen to anyone).

I heard a lot of news like people dying due to starvation. I thought, do people even die due to starvation?! I never believed it at an early age. It was just news for me. I overlooked it. (I shouldn't, my bad, I apologise).

During hours of road journey & due to some circumstances, I had no time and had to travel onward, so I proceeded without eating. After reaching Zurich, I felt so starved that I know the meaning of hunger, the true meaning of starvation. Believe me. I felt I'd die in the next moment. I touched that pain.

Right after reaching the destination, I called my mum (India). I don't remember, I apologised or no, I said, I will never skip my meals.

I realised how blessed we are! That we have food. We have a roof. Tap water. Clean water to drink. Nice clothes to wear. Varieties of healthy food that we can choose to eat

184

anything out of it, and school for education, family – a pillar of support, what else? I don't complain & I don't waste food. One incident changed my way of thinking about life.

My help and donations I love to keep confidential. I am not a great personality (as I too made loads of huge mistakes) to preach, but I would love to mention here, please help those in need (genuinely), especially the underprivileged. (if you can). If you don't want and can't help, still it's okay but at least act with kindness (I promise, it won't cost you a single penny). You don't know directly indirectly whom you will save with a ray of happiness and hope. After all, we are human, aren't we? Why can't we keep humanity alive?

I didn't cry that eve., maybe due to thinking something productive or something else. But I ordered my first pizza (yes, first pizza) in Zurich. It was delicious. I felt grateful.

Kills me or Cares for me

At one international airport, in the process of baggage check-in, all of a sudden someone touched her. She turned around to see. She was shocked.

She: Hey! After a long time

He: Yeah!

She: Did you miss me?

He: A lot

She: What made you miss me?

He: Five chocolates, everyday

She: I need seven now

He: No! Why did you leave me?

She: Our lives were different. And My dreams are everything to me.

He: It was nothing like that

She: I don't know, you hurt me a lot

He: Do you still have feelings for me?

She: I am sorry, but I never had feelings for you.

He: Why?

She: Cause I never told you, I was always committed to my dreams and goals. At that time, I was facing trauma. I had been resting from work a few times. Somewhere you saved me. I am grateful for that.

He: Then why were you with me for so long? Why fake promises? Why Fake care?

She: Honestly, I still can't forget the way your palm was trembling. It was all new to me. You were in pain. I was bound to be within my boundary.

He: Liar. You were using my time only.

She: Smiled ....mysteriously.

He: I know you are a liar, fake and whatnot. Why?

She: I used to lie because I didn't want to catch feelings for anyone, not even for you. I can't settle with any. I am like this, take it or leave it.

He: Come back?

She: No.

He: I will die.

She: I still don't care. I will keep you alive in my stories but never come back in your life.

He: Seriously!

She: Yeah! I know you don't like books & you won't bother to read them either.

He: You know hell a lot about me

She: No, don't overthink

He: Reason behind your anger?

She: You know better.

He: No, I don't know.

She: It's Okay

He: Love the way you used to care. I feel one of the luckiest men who got a chance to grab your attention.

She: Attention!

He: Well, yeah.

She: I am sorry, I hurt you a lot. You were the best part of my life. Trust me. But I can't come back to your life. I have to leave, take care & try to leave your addictions, cigarette and alcohol, not good for health.

She smiled and left forever.

He: I don't know if she cares for me or kills me through her beauty and grace.   *Whispered*

A Bowl of mashed potatoes

*T*hey were sitting at the beach. A best friend asked: What do you like about gifts?

She: Anything with love and…

He (Interrupted): She loves a beautiful pair of Magenta Pink Bangles.

She: How do you know that I love bangles!

She looked at him in aggression, asking, rolling her eyes.

He: I stalked your social media, where you mentioned it.

She: Lol! I didn't mention its colour.

He: Even I can tell you how many times you blink in 60sec. I know what you crave to eat.

She: What?

He: A bowl of mashed potatoes.

She: Woah! Concentrate on studies rather than PhD in me.

Their friend screamed. He silently loves you.

She: Not again! The only thing I don't know how to handle. *fainted due to shock*

Grammar Monk

He: Are you Grammar Nazi? He asked rudely.
She: No! A Grammar Monk. She replied proudly.

Thank you for the gift Sir!

On her 18th birthday

*H*e: Hey! I have got an expensive gift for you.

She: WOW! On cloud 9 (few sec. pause), but you are my senior and neighbour. Sir, I can't take anything from you. I respect you.

He: You are hurting me now.

He gave it too forcefully.

An innocent heart couldn't deny it out of respect. Hence received it and returned home.

He called on her phone.

He: Have you checked the gift box?

She: Not yet, Sir!

He: Go to your room and open it.

She: Sure! Sir,

He: Good Girl

She: It's too revealing! I don't wear dresses like this.

He: I don't care, wear it, click a picture and send me.

She: Sir, I can't. I respect you.

He: Then how dare to receive an expensive gift, if you can't do what I am saying? You used me. You pretend to be innocent, but are not.

She Lost her temper

She fiercely packed the dress back and dispatched it with a note, {Sir! Despite several denials, you gave me the gift box. A beautiful dress but too revealing. I received it out of respect without knowing your intention. Sir! What a tricky way to see my body. Next time, if you want to impress a girl, start it with your wife. She would admire it. I am just your neighbour. And if you again think to give me a gift on my birthday, give me colourful Bangles (Pride for a Girl). I would love to wear them with my dignity and honour. I just love bangles, not expensive gifts or too revealing attire.

Moreover, my would-be partner whom I will choose would deserve to spoil me with such gifts. I would love to receive it from him, only. The dress was beautiful, no doubt! I didn't need it.

If I choose not to return it because no one will come to know about it, I can't cheat my inner self, which I proudly keep pure. Sir! I finally got my voice. Thank you for the Gift. Sir!

Blushed

An Evening

She wore his favourite purple evening dress on a dinner date at one of his favourite places.

He: What do you want to order?

She: A cup of coffee and Ice tea.

He: Just coffee and Ice Tea! Babe! It's not our first date. We are here for dinner.

She: It all started with a cup of coffee and Ice Tea. I would love to have them again, together. I tried every possible thing to leave you and your place and to shift abroad. Whenever I tried, I got into more mess. As if the universe tells me to be with you only. I want to look back, how far we have come walking together. You didn't let me go anywhere and never gave up on me. Why?

He: I love the way you blush.

She smiled, gazed at the floor... *Blushed*

Meteor Star

*S*he came in a luxury brand new car, knelt, hands clasped and begging.

She: I Love you more than my life

He : *Smiled*

She: Why can't you accept my love?

He : *Silent*

She: Have you ever fallen in love?

He: Yeah, just once

She: Why did you break up?

He: Did I say this? We are still in love. She used to interact sitting next to me. Now I interact with her looking at the sky.

She: Lol! In this era such love exist?

He: Look at the sky once

She gazed at the sky. The meteor shower has started.

(Hashtag, true love exist)

A Surprised Musical Morning

The mobile screen flashes with notification received a voice note. Woah! It was one of her favourite songs. A fan sent to surprise her, as she was not keeping well for so long.

She wrote him a note.

I was overwhelmed this morning. I received a morning surprise in my message box when I heard my favourite song in his (a Fan) voice. I felt like "oh là là" (surprised).

What a talent! What a voice! As far as it was tough to sing as English is not our mother tongue. However, nothing is impossible for a genius.

It was one of my favourite songs. Thanks, champ! You made my morning.

The way She reciprocated

Do Boys Cry?

*A*t the study table, at midnight around 02:00 am, She took a small break from homework. Let's do social media. She checked the message box to see how many people are online to talk. There were not too many, but one good friend was online, she texts him.

She: Hi!

He: Still awake?

She: Yes, studies. Why are you still awake?

He: I was watching a video. It was so emotional that it made me cry.

She: What!

He: Why are you shocked? It was just a family video, not a creepy one.

She: I am shocked to know. Do boys ever cry?

He: Honestly, yes, they do

She: When did you last cry?

He: With tears or without tears?

She: Do you even have crying types?

He: Yes, we do have

She: Okay! So when did you cry last time with OR without tears? Tell me both.

He: With tears in December, time of winter, when my beautiful sister got married. And without tears, I cry quite often.

She: You are a gentleman. Real man. You have a heart. You dare to confront it.

He: Your posts are women-centric. It made me feel like you have some grudges with boys. Are you sick or what at this time?

She: I post on women-centric because I am a girl. But I never think anything wrong about boys, like you. You behave respectfully. I can see you don't even have a bad intention with me. We have been talking for almost a year. You never send anything wrong that made me uncomfortable. You have been raised good, so you know that most girls can't defend themselves. You didn't think to take advantage of my innocence. Even you helped me many times, selflessly. Our topics are always based on knowledge and foreign universities for higher education, so I feel comfortable talking to you like a good friend. A few chapters with few cheap people don't make all Men bad. I like it when a boy cries & pour emotions out. I respect it enough, because I know their lives aren't as easy as it seems. So chill. I don't have personal grudges with Boys if they are respecting and defending women in need.

He:*Sigh of Relief* I respect & defend women. But why can't they protect themselves?

She: Because we are cute & we can't fight like a Buoy.

He: I know *smiled*

Never criticize a book

On his 23rd Birthday

*H*e: What did you bring me on my Birthday?
She: A Book
He: Book! Didn't you find anything less boring?
She: It's handwritten.
He: Seriously! Are you jobless or what?
She: No! I was in love but with the wrong one.

She took the handwritten book along with her and returned home.

After eight months, she transformed handwritten into a well-published book about Business & Leadership and became a bestseller Author.

Her ex was still struggling between 9-5.

Never criticize a book. Writing a single page takes a whole day and night. A book binds solely with emotions and intelligence (a rare combination in making a BOOK). Don't judge a book by its cover. Respect the power of the book.

Ocean Drops

They threw me in an ocean. I came out becoming a swimmer.
They pushed me from the 20th Floor. I became a skydiver.
They put me on starvation. I became a skinny model.
They played mind games. I became the coach.
They tried to use my money. I became a philanthropist.
They tried to lure me with their wealth. I became a monk.

I woke up, looked at my surroundings, a grammar book staring at me and asked for a day off. The laptop was in agony and asked for the morning meal, a beautiful colourful pencil asking to sleep two more hours.

After 24hrs non-stop work.
I sent them on vacation for a day.

Lots of Love
KC

Grateful

Acknowledgements

My Guardian Angels on Earth in human form

Thank you, Papa: You taught me the value of health. To eat healthy food and live a healthy lifestyle. You keep health above all. My reason behind being fit is none other than you. One of the best memories with you is how we used to go to the library spending several hours reading books and newspapers. You are so intellectual, realistic, unpretentious. I respect you the most.

Beautiful Mamma: You have an extremely positive persona. Without your support and sacrifices, I wouldn't have been the person I am today. You are a true definition of beauty and motherhood. You taught me to live life without comparing myself to others. One should always feel blessed for whatever we have. I am grateful that you believe in me. Despite showing me the right direction, somewhere in my life, I lost my path; therefore, I feel regret and apologies. I know I had given you several wounds and hurt you the most. I apologise for neglecting your care and being adamant. I feel blessed to have you as my parent. The fact is, as you are already aware, you are the one I love the most.

Nils: I am grateful to you for making my childhood happening and perfect. I always respect you and admire you. Love you to the moon & back. You are precious to us. Hence never forget to smile & live your best. Thanks for giving us Hyan.

Bhai: You are my only reason for coming home. I would be incomplete without you. Thanks for admiring me a lot, your compliments, motivations whenever I feel empty and nervous. You are always there to give me a ray of hope. I failed at many stages in my life. Although you never let me give up, and whatever I do, you always trust my abilities. I appreciate your loyalty towards me. How adorable you are. I love the way you correct me.

Az: You believe in me. Every so often, I am astonished at the fact that you know me so well and take care of my every wish, whether it is worthy or undignified. You have always been there to protect me in unfavourable situations without pretending and showing off. You taught me the power of simplicity. The value of love and to look after our parents. Grateful for everything.

I feel blessed to have these people around me. Without all their support & love, I couldn't have taken a single step towards success in my life. I wouldn't have been an author if it weren't for you.

Soul, Chini, Mitthu & Kiwi (La Familia) – Love you always.

An Honour

Respected JRN – Your Bunto (My Mumma) misses you every day. So much respect to you & Family.

Respected Daata, Respected Ranisa - Maamaa & Family – Grateful for appreciating us & keeping Mumma motivated. So much respect to you & family.

Respected Maya Aunt: A die-hard fan of Mumma. I appreciate the way you dignify us and pamper me. Best wishes to you & your family.

She is My Favourite

Almond: Thanks for looking after lands. Your hard work even in the sunlight just to grow organic foods for us. A TEA *(can never forget that day)*. The way you call me 'Komal Baisa'. I am younger than you but with the respect you give me, I feel touched. *(I will surely find time and try my best to give you a mobile phone & travel on a flight together, one day)*.

Apart from the above, I would love to be grateful for everything towards **my essential family members:**

Respected Daddy: Grateful to teach me the term: Style. Nanisa: An epitome of care.

Maa: Thanks for introducing me to designer clothes (*A lot left unfinished*).

Lok M & Family – Appreciate your support to Mumma; thank you.

My Grandparents, my uncles, aunts & cousins – Thank You.

Grateful

All Teachers that shaped me.

All seniors, my roomies (Chandni, Jagriti - safeguarded me from Stella. Rashu - Thanks for cooking boiled food for me.)

All ex-employer that gave me beautiful work opportunities.

All my ex-colleagues were always there for me whether it was my own travel-related or work assistance.

Kudos

To My Legal advisor, Adv. Abhishek

To My Finance Handling

To My Book Club

Thank you, Team (Paper Towns India)
Marketing Team (The Bookoholics)

My journey of writing a book and being an Author would have never been completed if these people didn't work diligently on A Starry-Eyed. I would love to reciprocate their efforts.

The Bookoholic Team & Paper Towns India

Mr Narendra
Mr Manik
Ms Aditi (Cover designer)
Ms Khushboo, Chandni (Editor)
Ms. Neha

I am grateful. I apologise as I made you wait a year and a half with continuously changes in the manuscript and the book cover. It was a great learning experience for me.

Good Luck!

Thanks: All the delivery partners who hand over the book to my readers.

I respect everyone, so I consider every human being as God's Child. Even I want to apologize to all those people whom I hurt directly or indirectly. As far as I know, my intention was always right. I have no amount of grudges left against anyone. Forever Grateful to all. May God bless you always. Mercy.

_ Best Wishes

Indebted Forever - Mumma

You saw me when I opened my eyes for the first time. You listened to my first voice (I must have said-Maa), you were the eyewitness of my innocence and pure heart. You saw my first smile. You were still smiling when I ruined your new Saree with my shit when I was a newborn. You taught me my first baby step. You shared your Blood and Oxygen in the placenta. You sacrificed everything to give a smile.

After I grew up, I became an adult. I forgot everything and got busy fulfilling my dreams. I didn't look back to you how much you need me. You must have cried, missing me when I remained busy at work. I thought my dreams were everything. But I was wrong. You are everything for me. And Yes, Parents are allowed everywhere to come.

Mumma, could you please hide me in the placenta and connect me with an umbilical cord, once again? *The safest place, ever.*

Made in the USA
Monee, IL
15 July 2022